Riders on the Storm

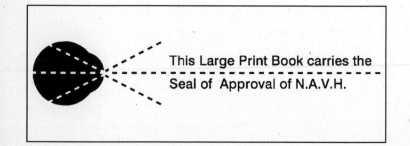

This Large Print Book carries the
Seal of Approval of N.A.V.H.

RIDERS ON THE STORM

ED GORMAN

THORNDIKE PRESS

A part of Gale, Cengage Learning

GALE
CENGAGE Learning®

Farmington Hills, Mich • San Francisco • New York • Waterville, Maine
Meriden, Conn • Mason, Ohio • Chicago

GALE
CENGAGE Learning®

LIBRARY OF CONGRESS CATALOGING-IN-PUBLICATION DATA

Gorman, Ed.
  Riders on the storm / by Ed Gorman. — Large print edition.
    pages ; cm. — (Thorndike Press large print mystery) (A Sam Mccain
mystery)
  ISBN 978-1-4104-7577-0 (hardcover) — ISBN 1-4104-7577-8 (hardcover)
  1. McCain, Sam (Fictitious character)—Fiction. 2. Private
investigators—Fiction. 3. Vietnam War, 1961-1975—Veterans—Fiction. 4.
Large type books. I. Title.
PS3557.O759R535 2015
813'.54—dc23
                                             2014042167

Published in 2015 by arrangement with Pegasus Books, LLC

Printed in Mexico
1 2 3 4 5 6 7 19 18 17 16 15

To my grandchildren:
Shannon, Patrick (PJ), Reagan,
Kate, Maggie, and Charlotte
With my profound love and respect

To some of the good ones
along the way:
Nancy Angenend, M.D.
Jennifer Berns, PA-C
Erin E. Brown, ARNP
Lynne (Russell) Conlin
Chad Davis, PA-C
David Dingli, M.D., Ph.D.
Larry Donner
Jill Flory, M.D.
Mark and Barb Johnson
Uva Mae (McAtee) Klein
Jean (Murrin) McNally, M.D.
Tammy O'Brien A MD
Tina Perry
Kevin and Deb Randle
Tracy Ridgeway, RN, BSN, OCN
Bill Schafer
Judy (Stevenson) Schneiderman

I'd like to thank
Penny Freeman, LISW
Tracy Knight, Ph.D., LP
Lt. Colonel Kevin Randle
for their invaluable help with this novel.

Once again I need to thank my friend and first editor Linda Siebels for her skill, her patience, and her humor. You're the best, kiddo.

Thanks to all the organizations dedicated to keeping those of us with the incurable cancer Multiple Myeloma alive as long as possible.

"Just as I was getting ready to fly home from Nam my sergeant told me not to wear my uniform, that a lot of us were getting hassled for wearing them. But I figured to hell with it. I fought in the war, didn't I? I was proud of my uniform. But when I got to O'Hare this kid, this girl who couldn't have been more than thirteen or fourteen comes running up to me and spits on me and screams that I'm a 'baby killer.' Her dad came over and dragged her away but man I could not fucking believe it. Thirteen or fourteen."

— Corporal Tom Squires

My name is Sam McCain. There was a time eight months ago when I didn't believe that. When both a neurosurgeon and a psychologist visited me every day and tried to convince me of it. With no luck for five weeks.

What happened to me was that I went to Fort Hood with four others from my National Guard unit to work on a special project our Guard captain thought would be good experience for us. You know how the Guard is in this piece-of-shit war we're having with Vietnam. King's X. Home Free. Got it made. You get in the Guard and the percentage of you going to Nam is very low. Very.

So one night we're all getting drunk (this was told to me) as we did every night we could and I don't know who brought it up but one of us said Shit, we should enlist. Look how many guys from our hometown of Black River Falls, Iowa, are over there already. And there have already been six deaths from our town since 1964. What kind of pussies are we, hiding out in the Guard?

We made this pact and somehow we remembered it in the morning and did exactly that. Went to this sergeant we'd met and said sign us up. A week later we got to go into town and do some drinking. I made the mistake of hitching an early ride back with a sergeant who was a lot drunker than I'd first realized. He piled up our Jeep by running into a tree going flat-out. He was killed instantly.

The neurosurgeon operated on me for almost fourteen hours. When I finally got out of surgery (again these are all things I was told) I had no strength, I had no memory except for these strange Poe-like images (Poe as in the Roger Corman drive-in movies which I loved). And except for the fact that some of these stray images scared me and some made me sad and some made me happy and some made me horny I had no real idea of what they meant. Had I just imagined them, or did they relate to this Sam McCain guy they kept telling me I was?

And after my memory returned I almost wished it hadn't. I was informed that my mom had had a stroke and was now living in Chicago with my little sister. And then I read the letter that my fiancée had written me while I was still not Sam McCain. I have to say that for a "Dear John" kind of thing she'd come up with a pretty good reason for ending our engagement. She'd told me that after her first husband died (in Nam in fact) she'd taken to drink and running around and sleeping around. She hadn't told me that she'd had a child and that rather than abort it (which she was inclined to do) her lover took it and raised it. She hadn't seen the man or her daughter since a few weeks after the birth. But they came back through town and — There you go.

The not having a memory thing isn't as bad as people sometimes think. For quite a while that was one memory I didn't want to have at all.

Finally I was released. I went immediately to Oak Park to see my mother who was living in this huge house. My sister's second husband not only didn't beat her up, he was nice enough to have money and even have one of the large empty rooms on the second floor turned into a small apartment for Mom. Her own bathroom even.

Then it was back to Black River Falls.

It turned out that the odd anxiety I felt as

I drove the Interstate was warranted.

The war was not only destroying people overseas, it was destroying them back in my hometown.

■ ■ ■ ■

PART ONE

■ ■ ■

"We should declare war on North Vietnam. We could pave the whole country and put parking strips on it, and still be home by Christmas."

— Ronald Reagan

1

Despite the panic in his voice I risk wheeling into a convenience store for coffee. Whatever crisis he is facing this time, I won't be much help if I'm this groggy. It is twenty-three minutes to two a.m. That dread I'd felt coming home? It is finally realized on this bleak, mysterious night.

A town like Black River Falls generally goes to sleep between ten and eleven except for the taverns and the three clubs where you can dance. A Quad City businessman, which is often synonymous with Mob, has tried to open both a XXX bookstore and a strip club in the past year. The whisper is that in the next six months or so city council members will give up fighting — the guy loves lawsuits — and allow the bookstore. No doubt night owls of a special species will flock to it.

Will Cullen lives in the wealthy area of town. His home is a sprawling yellow-brick house that has been here long enough to have creeping vines venerating the exterior walls. A piney windbreak to the east isolates the place from its neighbors. His wife Karen has a wealthy father who paid for the place. He thought that maybe this kind of splendor would help Will recover from his Nam tragedy.

I top a small hill and gaze down at the moonlit homes stretching out before me. Senators love to bluster about how the rest of the world envies us, and when you see this portrait in shadow and light you have to agree with them. Solid houses, good jobs, bright futures. Too bad we were losing thousands of our troops — not to mention even more thousands of innocents — just so two fine fellows named Johnson and Nixon could play John Wayne.

The streetlights are sparse and so my headlights and motor hum seem all the more intrusive as I sail down the street to Will's home.

I have my window rolled down. The slight chill feels good after the blistering August we've been having.

The enormous house is dark. Maybe Will hadn't wanted to wake Karen or their daughter up. Still, the dark house puzzles me and makes me uneasy.

I glide up the driveway and snap off the engine. The triple-stall garage is closed. His and her cars will be inside.

The scent of flowers — morning glories and scarlet rockets from what I can see in the deep shadows — lend the breeze a pleasant scent. The only other aroma is of the Lucky I am smoking.

I walk from my car up the curvy and lengthy flagstone path to the front door. I expect him to step out at any minute. I knock feebly, thinking of Karen and their three-year-old daughter Peggy Ann. No response.

There is a huge window to the right of the front door so I go over there and peer in. The faint light of the half-moon lends the living room the look of a showroom. There is a joke among all their friends that Karen is such a fastidious housekeeper she'd prefer that when you visit you stay outside. God help the person who sets a drink down without using a coaster. Death would be swift.

No sign of Will.

I have terrible thoughts. Every once in a while there are stories in the news about the lives of a seemingly happy family ending when the husband — usually the husband, though wives have done it, too — takes a gun and kills the wife, the kids and finally himself.

I think of the mental problems Will had developed while serving in Vietnam. Like many sufferers of post-traumatic stress disorder, he has turned to alcohol to deal with his griefs. Karen has told me that he's even started drinking at work sometimes. He has been put in mental hospitals for short stays twice.

I move along the side of the house. More flowers, more scents. Distantly the sounds of eighteen-wheelers on the highway; a lone lonely dog a few blocks over barking out his need for companionship.

I stop at the side door. People in our town of thirty-five thousand or so still leave their doors unlocked. This is slowly changing with the increase of serious crime across the country.

I try the door. Apparently Will is still of the belief that you can trust your neighbors. The door is unlocked.

I have terrible thoughts again.

If I call the police and there is nothing wrong — maybe Will has just had one of his frightening panic attacks — then I will have embarrassed Will. Karen is from some of the town's oldest money. She is the reason that Will's veterinary clinic is doing so well. She is on enough boards of this and boards of that to know people who do not mind expending heavy-duty dollars on their animals.

I start inside and then stop. A good way to scare the hell out of people; a good way for me to get shot. Both of them know how to shoot. Karen's father owned a large chain of sporting goods stores. The entire family was taught to shoot, even, and as Karen often joked, the dog.

I close the door and then stand in the starlight deciding what to do next. My impulse is to just get in my car and head back to my apartment.

Then I see the beam of a flashlight waving around inside in the kitchen window.

The light vanishes quickly. Through a window close to the front room I see the beam again still waving around. Searching for something.

Then the living room light comes on.

I move cautiously back to the front of the house and there she is in the window. Karen in a flattering pink nightgown, her mussed, bobbed blond hair giving her the look of a just woken child. But that impression is contradicted by the Colt Python in her hand. Pretty as she is, there is a hard side to her. I have no doubt she is tougher than Will.

When she finally sees me, she sets the gun down on the table and hurries to the front door. As she's letting me in she says, "Are you all right, Sam? What're you doing here?"

"Will called me. About twenty minutes ago."

"Will did? Why?"

"What I'm thinking now is that he must've

had one of his panic attacks."

We have a small circle of friends. We all know of Will's troubles. His panic attacks, the frightening temper he's developed, his inability to get a good night's sleep, his recklessness in both his personal and business lives.

"He always wakes me up when he has them. Usually I give him more of his meds and sit with him until he calms down. I wonder why he didn't wake me up tonight." Will had accidentally shot and killed a little girl in Nam. He's never gotten over it. And worst of all, sometimes he has to rush out of his own home when he sees his daughter, who is about the same age as the little girl he killed. Mere sight of Peggy Ann triggers all his self-loathing and terror. Drunk one night he told Karen that maybe their daughter is actually the little Vietnamese girl here to haunt him.

We are standing a few feet apart. She smells of sleep and yesterday's perfume. "I'm so sorry you had to come over here, Sam. Look at the time. You have to get up and go to work in a few hours."

"And Peggy Ann will have you up pretty early yourself."

"Is there something I can get you? How about a beer?"

"I won't say no."

She pats me on the cheek. "You're such a

good friend, Sam. I'll get you your beer and then round up Will. He may be embarrassed and hiding in the den. He does that sometimes."

The living room is so formal I never quite feel comfortable in it. From the grand piano to the white-brick fireplace to the long flocked drapes that cover the tall narrow windows to the bay window that overlooks the swimming pool — I am always careful when I'm here. I like the Cullens very much, it's just that their modest abode is a little less modest than my own. I sit down on a tan leather ottoman, mindful that I don't want to brush my Levi's against her couch or chairs.

The beer is served in a fancy Pilsner glass. I thank her for it and she rushes off.

I soon hear a door open quietly. From here I can see into the hall that divides the house. A light comes on and then goes off almost immediately. A child's voice, frightened. Maybe a bad dream. Or adults up at this time of night. Adults do terrifying things at night. Even three-year-olds know that.

Karen has a soothing voice and she uses it now with her daughter. I can't understand the words but the sound Karen makes is almost songlike. There will be hugs and kisses and then Peggy Ann will be tucked back down into the gentle dreams of three-year-olds. She will forget whatever had woken her.

Karen comes back. Shaking her head and twisting her long hands together. "He's not in the den or any of the bathrooms or the kitchen. Just a second. I should try the basement."

"Let me try that, Karen. Why don't you just sit down?"

I am pretty sure she knows as well as I do that he isn't in the basement. Not unless he's dead down there. At his own hand.

I spend several minutes in the basement. It is not only finished but also furnished with expensive family room chairs and a couch. There is even a small bar and a twenty-nine-inch TV console. Even though I am not much of a sports fan — except for the World Series — I've spent many long afternoons down here with Will's group of vets.

She waits for me at the top of the stairs. She's changed into dark slacks and an olive-colored cotton blouse. Her feet are in thongs.

"No luck?"

"Sorry. No luck."

She waits until the basement door is closed again before she says, "Now I'm afraid, Sam."

"Before either of us starts to panic, let me check the garage, which I should have done first anyway. I'm just a little foggy, I'm afraid."

"You think he went somewhere? It wouldn't be like him to go anywhere. After he has these attacks he usually goes to sleep and I have a hard time waking him up."

"I'll flip the backyard light on and go have a look."

"I'd like to go with you." Tension has tightened her narrow face.

I smile. "Since it's your house I think that can be arranged."

The backyard grass is green and rich in the sudden light. A picnic table, a child's swing set, a barbeque are spread across the sizable stretch of yard. Suburban bliss.

She keeps so close to me she bumps me a few times.

I've known Will since we made our First Communion together. He'd been one of those kids who didn't take much seriously. B's were fine with him. His main interest until late in high school was science fiction in all forms. He'd had a few dates but none had ever turned into anything serious. In his sophomore year in college he'd shocked everybody by going out with a true heartbreaker, Cathy Vance. There were a lot of jokes about how he'd managed to get her to fall in love with him, including mind control. Two years they went together and when it ended it was him not her who broke it off. They were engaged until he suddenly met Karen. They got married quickly and had Peggy Ann four months after the rings slid on their fingers. Then he was drafted. Before the war he'd been the dominant one. When he returned, their relationship changed considerably. He'd come home in pieces and shards of his former self.

Before the war they'd been parents and friends. But given his condition on returning she'd also had to become mother, sister, protector, and defender. Anybody who'd thought she was just a rich girl and a snob had to quickly and forever change their minds. Her love for him was fierce and resolute.

She carries the garage door opener with her when we walk outside. Now she thumbs it and we wait and listen as the door rumbles. As we start inside I can see that the stall for Will's Thunderbird is empty.

2

You don't expect to find a sitting senator and a couple of reporters at a backyard barbeque. That was my first thought last night when I showed up at Tom Davis's new native stone and glass home on a perch above the river.

I might have been happier to see a senator if he hadn't been one who was hawkish on the war but had two draft-eligible sons who had mysteriously not served. He was a proud friend of the defense industry and, as *Time* had leaked to no apparent avail, a heavy investor in said industry. Though he was a Republican, he wasn't friendly with our brave and laudable Republican governor who had denounced the war last year.

The press was there — a TV crew from Cedar Rapids and an old-time newspaper reporter from here in town — so I assumed this was the night that Senator Patrick O'Shay was going to announce that he had persuaded Steve Donovan to run for the Congressional seat in this district. O'Shay needed some help. His opponent was now in a virtual tie with the lordly Mick.

I would stick to beer. Since my return from the military hospital I'd taken to getting sloppy drunk sometimes. I didn't want to inflict this on what was supposed to be a gathering of Nam vets.

Fifty or sixty people fitted comfortably on the breathtaking patio from which you could see across the river to where the white birch trees showed ghostly in gloom. Rain was in the forest and you could smell it and taste it but it didn't seem imminent.

I would have brought Mary, but ten days ago I'd told her that it was all moving too fast and that I was confused and that the meds weren't tempering my anger or my depression. They also weren't helping in the erection department. One out of six or seven times I couldn't get it up. The docs said this might happen. As if that was any comfort.

She hadn't cried when I made my announcement. She'd had a notably tough life and accepted it quietly. All she said was that the girls would miss me. I loved all three of them equally, if in different ways. Kate and Nicole were a lot more fun than anything on TV. I hadn't actually moved in. I'd stayed late, but always went back to my apartment.

The headache came about a half hour after I got there. Stress. The docs said that because of the two neurological operations I'd had, my moods would sometimes be difficult for me and for those around me. I felt out of place here, but then I felt out of place just about everywhere since coming back home.

I used one of the four bathrooms in the lavish house and dumped two capsules down me. Generally they'd back down the headache within an hour.

It was time for me to do the social thing.

I shook a lot of hands; I laughed and flattered and remained staunchly humble when people talked about how brave I'd been. Brave? Some drunken sergeant piled up a Jeep I happened to be riding in; nothing brave about that. And I had a shit-eating smile that could charm a mass murderer. Maybe I could give O'Shay some pointers on peddling his ass. A few of the more observant ones said I'd changed. They could sense it, feel it, and they weren't just talking about the inch-long scar that ran just under my hairline.

All the vets were from our county so we all pretty much knew each other's stories.

But there were a few who still wanted to know mine.

So many of the wives here tonight looked so sweet and loving and beautiful in the sentimental glow of the Japanese lanterns.

A couple of times I was tempted to ask for a drink from the pert young woman serving them from the silver impromptu bar near the west edge of the patio. But I stuck to slow-drinking my bottle of Hamm's.

The TV crew interviewed a number of couples. How did it feel to be home and safe? How many sleepless nights did you have knowing your husband was in harm's way? And then the question that had become controversial the last few days: What do you, as a soldier who fought over there, think of this anti-war group of soldiers led by a man named John Kerry?

There was a mix of responses. Anger (which is what the crew wanted); sadness (knowing that vets would turn on each other this way); understanding. The two vets who opted for this spoke specifically of one vet, the local vet who'd signed up for the group, Will Cullen.

"Will's my friend," said a brawny vet named Max Kirchoff. "He's had problems dealing with the war and I wish some of the fellas would take that into account. He went

34

over there and served along with the rest of us. I don't agree with this anti-war thing but if it makes Will feel a little better about himself, I'm all for it."

"Will's like family to us," his petite wife said.

This explained why Will wasn't here tonight. Probably better than half of the other vets would be happy to see him. They were like Kirchoff. Guy went over there and suffered a breakdown. Did two stints in mental hospitals. He's not thinking straight so he signs on to this dumb-ass anti-war group.

On the other hand there were the vets like soon-to-be Congressional candidate Steve Donovan. He'd been interviewed on TV yesterday and said that the anti-war group was not only "a disgrace but also run by Communists." He added: "I know there's a vet right here in town who's joined. I'd be very careful if I were him. A lot of us here resent him a hell of a lot."

So Will and Karen stayed home.

The speechifying started right at seven thirty. There would still be time to get the story on the ten o'clock news in Cedar Rapids.

Tom Davis thanked everybody for being here tonight. He talked sincerely about the

35

special bond vets had. And then he toasted them. Hard as you tried to hate him for his inherited wealth, his acumen as a business-man, his good looks, and his movie-star gorgeous wife, the sonofabitch wouldn't let you. He was just too nice a guy. I've learned to my dismay that there are a lot of down-right decent wealthy people. Not fair at all.

Now it was time for the commercial.

Patrick O'Shay had once been called "the biggest hambone in the Senate." If that had been an exaggeration, it was only slightly so. Tall, lean, white-haired, his body and its language suggested a mercenary side that belied the treacle that he usually spewed.

The Treacle Master proceeded.

"I'm so grateful to have been asked here tonight. To see the proud and happy faces of those who made the ultimate patriot's sacrifice — to fight for the freedoms we all enjoy in this country; the freest country in the history of the world. And I might say the same for the wives and children who waited for their brave warriors to return home. Ladies, I salute you tonight right along with your husbands."

As I glanced around I wondered what the men without legs, arms, sight were think-ing. Certainly they must have had second thoughts about the war. Had they realized

36

that it was nothing more than rich old men and the corrupt Pentagon living out another round of endless and pointless slaughter?

A few of the wounded men smiled — one man gave the thumbs-up with his right hand; he had no left hand — but the faces of their wives were solemn. One woman grimaced. O'Shay bullshit overload.

He went on, a little history for the groundlings:

"From the beginning of time women have waited for their men to come home from battle. As a proud Irishman I can tell you that the literature of my people is steeped in stories and poems about war. Nobody wants it, of course. I would never have voted for what we're doing in Vietnam if I hadn't seen the facts — that we have no choice but to stop them there before they come over here. And so the men fight and the women — the very good women just like the women here tonight — wait."

He blathered on another ten minutes before getting down to it. Easy to tell that he was enjoying it more than his constituents were.

"You know what this country needs more than anything right now? I'm sure you already know the answer to that. This country needs patriots. Real patriots. Not the kind who go overseas and fight and then return home to claim that what they did was morally wrong. There's a sickness in our society that breeds men like this —"

The applause surprised me. Close to half the group clapped. A few whistled.

"But I didn't come here tonight to belittle anybody. I came here tonight to say that with your help we can put a true man and a true patriot in this Congressional seat — and I don't have to tell you who that is, do I? A very successful businessman as well. Come over here, Steve!"

This time everybody applauded. I joined in. He was a shit most of the time but then there was a decent, generous side to him that almost, but not quite, made you like him. I'd known him since grade school. He'd always been this way.

Donovan was a slick package. A fit, blond man who'd played good basketball at the university in Iowa City, he'd just gotten his business launched when Uncle Sam dragged him out of his house. Tonight he was dressed much like the senator. Golf shirt, in his case black; tailored yellow slacks; a large and no doubt real gold watch; and a smile that could not quite hide the smirk inside.

My eyes strayed to his wife Valerie, who stood at the front. A perfect fit for him. A lithe brunette of brutal beauty in a chic emerald fitted dress and a smile very much like hubby's. Practiced and cold. She applauded just the right, proper way and gazed just the right, proper way on our next congressman. The too liberal for these times — and face it, uninspired — congressman presently holding the seat would undoubtedly stay in Washington, but now as consultant or lobbyist.

"Those of you who know me know that I'm not really practiced at giving speeches. Valerie and me" — the classic ungrammatical pronoun to go along with this whole shuck and jive I'm just a regular feller bullshit — "we're private folks. So this doesn't come natural to me."

"You do great!" a man in the back shouted.

"Well, thank you. I appreciate the support. And I'll need that support when I run."

The orgasm moment. He's running. Applaud until your hands run with blood; scream until you lacerate your throat.

The camera man — a young guy interchangeable with most hippies you saw on the street — panned the faces of the excited people up front.

Donovan started waving for them to calm down, but that smile said who could blame them? A hot-shit property like me? Just who the hell *could* blame them?

"I'll tell you what, my friends. I'm going to accomplish things when we get to Washington. I'm going to cut the terrible taxation we all suffer under and I'm going to make sure that every single country on this planet is either our friend or our enemy. And if they're our enemy then all I've got to say is — watch out! I'm sick of hearing this country denigrated by all these third-rate loudmouths. And it's happening right here at home. Just look at our morals. Moral people can't go to movies anymore. And the songs on the radio. I'm not afraid of censorship. You heard me say that, right? Sometimes you have to have censorship. And one more thing — I won't let any so-called American citizen run this country down. And that goes for soldiers who sign petitions that claim that our honorable service was immoral!"

I couldn't take any more applause. I let my bladder lead me into the house. When I finished I put the lid down and sat on it. I smoked and did a little smirking myself. I knew just enough about politics to know that he had to use groups like these to get the initial support he needed. When he started appearing before large groups he'd have to be much more moderate. The TV news tonight would be kind to him. He'd get at most a minute and a half and the sound bite would be how he was going to make our country safe again from porno and songs of sex. He sounded good; he looked good, didn't he? And who among the voters gave a shit anyway? He was as much against hippies and lust as they were, wasn't he?

I sat there a while longer, enjoying the fact that my headache was fading. I was tempted to call Mary, but what would I say? If I said I was lonely she'd interpret that as meaning that the break was over. But I needed the break.

I had left a patio loud and ripe with good times. But when I returned it sounded as if the party was winding down. It wasn't even eight thirty yet.

A beer sounded good but first I wanted to find out what was going on. I noticed that the crowd had split into smaller groups of fives and sixes. And I noticed they were talking quietly but earnestly.

What the hell was going on?

Then I heard the voices erupt from around the east wing of the house. I recognized Will's voice first. Then Donovan's. Donovan was drawing down on Will and Will was meekly trying to tell Donovan that he still wanted to be friends with all the vets. That his decision to sign the anti-war petition was nothing personal. I felt sorry for him then. There was no way that most of the vets would not take it personally. I understood that; apparently Will didn't.

And then they appeared on the patio.

My stomach churned. Sometimes the three different meds I took backed up in me but I didn't think this was the meds. It was these feelings of anger and sorrow and defeat that were so common these days. Will just looked so damned sad and played out and confused.

Donovan was dragging him. It almost looked like an old TV comedy routine. Donovan had Will by the collar of his button-down shirt while Will's arms were trying to push against Donovan. Will kept saying, "These're my friends, Steve. At least let me talk to them."

This was the scene Senator O'Shay returned to from somewhere inside the house. He must have been using one of the four bathrooms, too.

He commandeered the patio instantly. "Steve, stop it! What're you trying to do to this man?"

But Donovan was too angry to stop. His

face was ruby and sweat drained off him. "This is Cullen, the guy who signed the anti-war thing! He snuck around the side of the house! I'm just escorting him out!"

O'Shay advanced. Not too difficult to understand why he, too, was angry. But not at Will, at his protégé. Donovan had sounded too angry on his first on-camera appearance tonight but he could slide past it. But dragging somebody — even an anti-war vet — out of the party . . . O'Shay knew the rules. You could be a lot of things and hold a Congressional seat, but you could not be a madman.

O'Shay had to be reading the crowd as well. While maybe a fourth of the people shouted agreement with Donovan's rage, the majority looked unhappy and some looked disgusted. They knew Will as a mild, quiet man; they knew Donovan as a charming but dangerously short-fused man.

O'Shay reached out to grab Donovan much as Donovan had grabbed Will. But instead of releasing Will, Donovan launched into a real beating. Before O'Shay even had a chance to stop him Donovan pounded punches into Will's face and stomach and then started all over again. Blood spurted from Will's nose and the roll of his eyes indicated that he was unconscious before he hit the flagstone floor.

By now I and five other men had surrounded Donovan and forced him to stop throwing punches. His entire body surged with his fury. He screamed over and over that he wanted to kill Will.

Many women and more than a few men watched all this in fear and revulsion.

Donovan got his shirt torn in the process of the manhandling it took to hold him back. He raved on. He'd never been like this before the war; not this kind of lunacy. I would've heard about it.

Slowly, reason came back into his eyes. Not apology or shame but common sense. He gaped around as if he'd just been dropped here from another planet. You could see him begin to recognize not only faces but context. Maybe he wasn't sorry for what he'd done to Will but it was easy to see that he was embarrassed about it.

O'Shay was at the bar. I'd glimpsed him earlier flirting with the woman running it. Not flirting this time. When he got his drink he gunned it in a gulp and then held the glass out for a refill.

No doubt his people had vetted Donovan and no doubt they'd learned of his temper and no doubt they'd weighed that temper against his points as a businessman and

Nam vet. But temper in the abstract is not the same as stories witnessed in real time.

O'Shay was in a dilemma. His people could minimize this with the press. Area reporters would not be eager to take on a war vet, particularly one who was also a prominent businessman. Maybe he could slide by this whole night. But what about the future?

I knelt next to Will. A woman who identified herself as a nurse joined me. She checked his vitals — not what they should be — and then checked his nose — not broken — and then she said the best thing would be to get him to an ER. He'd been savagely beaten.

His eyes fluttered open and he said, "I kicked his ass, huh?" He loved jokes. But then, his mood swings worse than mine, he started crying. The nurse took one arm and I took the other and we gradually got him sitting up.

A large number of people encircled us. Even a few vets I recognized as friends of Donovan were saying sympathetic things. Maybe Donovan wasn't such a hero to them anymore.

Just after I stood up a large sinewy hand fell on my shoulder. When I turned around I looked into the wary green eyes of O'Shay.

45

"I'm very sorry about this."

"I'm sure you are. He's one hell of a candidate."

"War vets are often stressed to the point of anger. I'm sure someone in the VA can deal with his anger problem."

Right now O'Shay was doing his own public relations. I couldn't dispute that Donovan was a brave man. He had the medals to prove it.

"I need to get Will to the hospital."

"We're here to help you," a vet I recognized from Iowa City said. "We'll help you get him in your car and we'll follow you all the way to the ER."

But O'Shay wasn't quite finished. "Someone pointed you out to me. Told me what happened at boot camp. I'm very sorry. If there's anything I can ever do for you, please let me know."

This guy could kiss your ass under water.

He turned away. He had a lot of work to do. He had to sell this crowd on what a great guy his seriously disturbed Congressional candidate really was.

Right now that was going to be one hell of a job.

3

We were talking about shunning.

There was an Amish community not too far from here and one of its rare but controversial practices was to shun a member who had violated certain beliefs or rules of the sect. They pretend the shunned person does not exist.

So Karen and I sat in the ER waiting area and smoked our cigarettes and kept glancing at the large round clock above the ER desk. As if checking it would hurry the intern who was examining Will. Karen had called a neighbor, who was now watching Peggy Ann.

On the way over here Karen had told me about some threatening letters that had been sent to their house over the last three months. Each looked like a kidnap note and each hinted at an ominous future. These really needed to be looked into.

She'd also told me about other letters.

"About a month ago I was cleaning his den and I found this shoebox on the shelf of the closet. It was pushed way back. I couldn't help myself. I took it down and opened it. There were all these love letters he'd written and never sent. Longhand, the tiny way he writes. He's been seeing Cathy Vance again." No tears; dead cold voice.

Cathy Vance was the college sweetheart he'd been engaged to, but he'd thrown her over when he met Karen.

Then we were in the Emergency Room.

Tart smells of medicine, hospital sounds including whispery calls over the intercom now that most of the patients would be sleeping or trying to, and the whoosh of the double ER doors as people passed in and out. I'd dated an ER nurse for a time and learned some things about the department. It was the Wild West. You never knew who or what you were going to get. One night a man with a gun had confronted her, demanding to see his estranged wife whom he'd just beaten half to death. Fortunately, in his rage and rush he hadn't noticed the police officer behind him. The officer had just brought in a drunk who'd fallen and cut his head. The officer now walked up behind the crazed husband and managed to take away the man's gun without incident.

48

"He used that word 'shunned' more than a few times in the past few days," Karen said. "You know he can be pretty dramatic sometimes but I know that's how he was feeling. Being in the army made him feel accepted as a man. He was afraid to go but I always sensed he thought he could prove something to himself over there. I don't think he ever felt adequate about being tough. God, I love him so much. I tried to warn him that this would happen if he signed that petition. Look what's going on in Washington."

A small faction of the anti-war vets (whose large numbers were being disputed by some in the press) had clashed at a demonstration with regular vets near the White House the other day. All the expected name-calling and bitterness. A particularly sad day for the country, I thought. A feast for the blowhards in Congress who loved to pout over alleged heresy.

"Then when he left tonight for the party —"

"He just said that he needed to buy oil, so —"

I smiled. "Oh, right. He learned how to change oil when he was over in Nam —"

"So he worked on his car whenever he could. It was another thing that made him feel good about himself."

A heavyset middle-aged Negro came in with his wife. She pointed to a chair and said, "Sit there, Bob. I'll get you all checked in." He wore a Cubs T-shirt and jeans. The way he gritted his teeth and held his right arm as if it was an infant suggested that he had broken it.

"He's in this softball league at work and he tried to slide into second base earlier tonight," she told the woman at the desk. She glanced back at him. "He thinks he's still sixteen, I guess. Anyway, we went home after the game but the pain's getting worse and worse."

The man had smiled at her when she'd said he thought he was still sixteen. He knew she'd been telling him that she loved him.

Our doc came along just as the woman was taking a seat next to her husband.

Will looked stronger and more purposeful than I'd expected he would. He'd been in the examination room for nearly an hour.

The intern was short, wiry, and balding. He had an O'Shay smile. He was going to send Will and Karen home happy. Maybe he'd give Will a sucker.

"The beating looked a lot worse than it actually was, Mrs. Cullen. There's no concussion, no fractures, just a whole lot of bruising. Warm baths will help that." He spoke to her as if Will was her child and not her husband.

She didn't wait.

She stepped over to Will and stood on tiptoe so she could kiss him. Will threw his arms around her and drew her in.

"He'll be much better in a few days," the intern said to me.

Karen wasn't about to let go of him.

"I'm writing two prescriptions for him, Mrs. Cullen. They'll help with the pain. They may make him a little groggy so I'd keep an eye on him."

"You don't have to worry about that." Karen beamed in relief.

Then we were outside in the steamy night. The mosquitoes were doing their version of the Normandy invasion. The three of us were the Germans. An ambulance about a quarter block from the ER external entrance had just cut its siren and emergency lights and speed so it could slot in right next to the ER double doors.

"This is actually kind of embarrassing," Will said. "I had a couple drinks and then I got this bright idea that I'd go out to the party and explain myself to all my friends and they'd all see that I wasn't this terrible

51

guy after all and then we'd all be buddies again. You know, like it is on TV when everybody is hugging each other after some big misunderstanding. I could write that crap myself." Grinning. He'd always been self-deprecating. One of the reasons we'd been friends is that we knew we hadn't been blessed with most of the gifts All-American Boys had been. Better to put yourself down than have somebody else do it for you.

Karen had a kiss for me. I tried not to notice how warm and soft her breasts felt against my chest. Or the scent of her hair. Or the simple pleasure of her affection for me. It would be so easy to call Mary.

"I'm scared, Sam, I'm really scared."

Karen stares at the empty stall normally filled with Will's cherry 1957 red Thunderbird. They'd joked that this would be both his Christmas and birthday gift until 2198. T-Birds in this kind of condition are not easy to find no matter what kind of coin you have.

The time according to my three-dollar-and-ninety-five-cent Timex is now two thirty.

"Did he come to bed last night?"

"I'm pretty sure he didn't. The covers weren't thrown back or anything. He didn't give you any hint he was going somewhere?"

"Our whole conversation was about a

minute. He just pleaded with me to come over and see him. Help him."

She puts long, thin hands over her face and inhales deeply. Then exhales. Then takes her hands away. "A drink and a cigarette. C'mon."

The kitchen is modern with gleaming white appliances, a parquet floor and a butcher block set up in the middle of the room.

We sit there for the next half hour waiting for the phone to ring or the noise of a motor to stir the silence of the driveway. He will be home. He will be safe. He's had another panic attack. He is such a fuck-up, will we please forgive him this one last time.

He doesn't call and he doesn't come home.

We decide, being medical experts, that the fight had concussed him after all. Doctors make mistakes and this intern — whom we'd never actually liked or thought much of when you came right down to it — this young doc is as full of shit as the machines they'd used on poor Will. The whole hospital is full of shit. And now here he is brain-damaged and wandering around and where is the intern right now? Probably having one of the night nurses give him a blow job in one of the storage rooms.

You know how you get when you desperately need to blame somebody.

Karen gets so riled she is going to call her

lawyer right now and institute a lawsuit for at least two hundred million dollars. Or more, dammit — more even.

Peggy Ann comes out in her little blue nightie to break our hearts. She stands there rubbing her eyes and asking how come Mommy and Daddy aren't in bed. She's had a bad dream and ran into their room for comfort but neither one of them was there.

"How come Uncle Sam is here?"

"He was working late and stopped by to say hello."

"It's dark out. How come he works when it's dark?" Way too smart for us.

"I had to help a friend of mine find his dog."

"We had a dog once. He ran away to be with his brothers and sisters." Woofer had been hit by a truck. The saving lie parents become experts at.

Karen goes over and picks her up and says, "I'm going to put her back to bed, Sam."

The temptation is to call the police. Our laughable chief of police, due to popular demand, had been summarily retired six months ago. His family owns and runs this town. But even they had to concede that he'd botched one too many cases. They'd imported a homicide detective from Peoria to take over the chief's job. He was reported to be quiet and competent, quite the contrast to Cliffie

54

Sykes, Jr., who'd dressed like Glenn Ford in Ford's Western movies — khaki with a campaign hat, don't you know — and who at his worst made even little children laugh.

I can call the station and ask for the three night cars to keep a cop eye out for Will in his red T-Bird. They'll be happy to do it and they'll likely find him without much problem. The trouble is, I don't know where Will is or what he's up to. Given everything that has happened tonight I have the feeling that much worse is possible. I'd been an H. P. Lovecraft fan in high school. I knew all about the dark gods and the enjoyment they take from destroying our lives.

"I took a trank," Karen says when she comes back. "I probably shouldn't have with the two drinks I had but right now I don't give a damn."

"I thought about calling the police."

"Why don't you?"

"He could be just driving around. He might not like being stopped by the cops."

"Please, Sam. We need to find him. And right away."

The call doesn't take long. A helpful officer — the new Chief Foster has replaced all of Cliffie's kin and buddies with officers who'd gone through the police academy and who didn't think that forensics was for sissies — knows of Will and has seen the T-Bird around

55

and will let all three cars know that they should be watching for him.

"That makes me feel better, Sam."

"I should've done it earlier. I guess I'm just punchy."

"You look exhausted."

"I was in court at nine this morning, meaning I had to be in my office by seven doing paperwork. Same thing tomorrow."

She is up and pecking me on the cheek. "I really appreciate you being here. You're the best friend either of us has ever had."

"You hear anything, call me."

"Even if I wake you up?"

"Even if you wake me up."

Sleep-hungry as hell, I head for my car.

4

When the phone rang on the small table next to my bed I wasn't sure I had the energy to reach for it. Sleep was such a wonderful mistress and now I was being wrenched from her arms by some interloper. Then I realized that it might be Karen and I shot straight up and grabbed the receiver.

"Sam, this is Paul Foster down at the police station. I know this is one hell of a time to be calling anybody, but something's come up I could use your help with."

The window was pink and gold, dawn. I had to pee real bad. And Tasha the cat had appeared to rub her cool nose against my arm. And I was eyeing my Luckies with great desire.

But couldn't these details be part of a dream?

Since when did the police chief of Black River Falls call on me for some help?

But dream or not, my presence was required.

"Yes, Chief."

"I know you're a good friend of Will Cullen's and Will's had a bit of trouble and I'd like to tell you about it."

"Uh, could you tell me a little bit more?"

"I don't blame you for wanting to know more but his wife Karen is here, too, and she needs a friend."

"I'll be there in fifteen minutes."

I was.

Chief Foster had redecorated Cliffie's old office. Instead of the John Wayne poster and framed photos of Cliffie all got up as Glenn Ford in various poses, the wall featured posters highlighting what it takes to be a competent police officer. A slight man, he was dressed in a summer-weight blue suit straight off the rack at Sears. I knew that because I had one just like it in a lighter blue. The thinning hair was combed from the right and the narrow, thin face showed intelligence and even reflection.

"I apologize for waking you up again, Sam, and please call me Paul."

Different strokes, as the song said. The laid-back style; hell, the apologies and the sensible clothes — Cliffie would have shot him on sight. I didn't like it much either. I don't hate cops, I don't love cops. But I do distrust cops. "Paul" invited the kind of intimacy that can be dangerous unless you happen to be another cop.

"Coffee?" He indicated a brewer on top of a gray metal bookshelf.

"Please."

After I'd sat down and after he handed me my cup, he sat down, too, and said, "There's a good possibility that Will Cullen murdered Steve Donovan last night." Then, "And from everything I know about Cullen I'd say that it's a pretty sad thing. I know he accidentally killed a little girl in Nam and has never really gotten over it. I was over there in '68. One tour and back home. I had a couple of buddies who re-upped. They both got killed. I'm telling you this so you understand that I have some sympathy for your friend. But I'm also a law enforcement officer so I have to do my job."

I'd been right to distrust him. Talk about a rush to judgment.

"Look, Chief, no offense, but you're way down the road here. Way down. I've known Will most of my life. He did not kill anybody."

He dismissed me. "I'd appreciate it if you'd let me do my job."

He started doing his job by telling me what he knew so far. Donovan had been drinking most of the night at a place called "Cherie's," an upscale roadhouse near the county line. Foster had talked to the manager of the place already this morning. He'd been there all night and said that Donovan had been very drunk but not belligerent. He got even worse when Will went out there and tried to talk to him. That sure as hell hadn't helped. They tried to talk Donovan into letting somebody drive him home but he got so pissed off the manager finally caved in.

As yet there were no witnesses to what happened next, or to what Foster assumed happened next. The place was so crowded so early last night that Donovan had been forced to park in a poorly lighted spot near the forest that ran up to Cherie's property line. When Foster looked over the scene this morning he found that both of Donovan's rear tires had been slashed. Foster's surmise was that when Donovan had drunkenly bent over to check on the tires somebody had smashed him over the head with a tire iron.

"How do you know it was a tire iron?"

"I'll get to that. Anyway, a jogger found the body. He cuts through the parking lot every morning to get on a nature trail about a quarter mile from there.

"Now the tire iron. About a block from the roadhouse there's a small rest stop. Will pulled in there. One of our patrol cars saw this Thunderbird sitting there and remembered that you'd called about it last night. He checked on the driver who he guessed was sleeping one off. He found the tire iron on the back seat. Bloody, with hair on it. The tire iron is in the forensic lab right now. The driver wasn't responsive in any way. The officer took him to the ER, where he's being examined."

I did my best not to look stunned by his claim about the tire iron. The back seat. Hair and blood. How could it get any worse?

"He was just in the ER last night."

"Yes, they mentioned that."

"I don't believe he killed Donovan."

"Neither does his wife."

"But you believe he did."

"You have to admit the circumstances could lead to that conclusion."

"Circumstances. Rather than evidence."

When I didn't say anything more, he said, "Pretty damn convincing evidence." Then, "You work for Judge Whitney as well as yourself?"

"Yes. You've met her?"

"She invited me to have dinner at her club

61

the other night. She's quite the woman. Was she really married four times?"

I nodded.

"And she used to play golf with Dick Nixon and she knows Leonard Bernstein well enough to call him 'Lenny'?"

I nodded again. He was changing the subject. I said, "Will didn't kill Donovan."

"I guess the record's stuck. I say there's a more-than-even chance he did. And I have some evidence to back up what I say. You, on the other hand, just keep saying he's innocent, but you don't have any evidence at all."

"I haven't had time to find any."

His lips thinned. "His wife is waiting for you down the hall, McCain."

Her package of Winstons had been ripped apart. I guessed she'd tried to open them but they wouldn't cooperate so instead she took all her anger out on the trim red package. Two cigarettes lay broken like snapped legs.

The room was twice the size of a cell. A wooden table and four wooden chairs comprised the furnishings. On a metal bookcase sat a tape recorder and a stack of Scotch recording tapes.

"I've never said the word 'fuck' in my life

but I've been saying it to myself ever since Paul called." Then, "Listen to me. The man arrested my husband for a murder he didn't commit and I'm calling him Paul. I should be calling him a fucker or something like that."

The relentlessly fastidious Karen was gone and in its place sat a disheveled woman whose loveliness had been robbed by lack of sleep, exasperation, and fear. There was a fresh stain on the right cuff of her sand-colored blouse. Probably from the coffee she was drinking now. She had affected a chignon but hairs sprang out like wings everywhere. She was without makeup. She'd probably been too upset to try an operation that delicate.

"At least they got rid of the death penalty in this state," she whispered.

I reached out and hugged her to me. I put my hand on the side of her face to bring her in even closer. I kissed the top of her head. She needed to cry and she did.

It was several minutes before she was able to gather herself and separate from me. She nodded down at her sundered cigarette pack and laughed tearily. "I guess I showed *them* who's boss."

"They had it coming."

"If you ever have a pack that gives you

trouble, let me handle them." Then, "He really didn't do it, Sam."

Our fervent mantra.

"And now," she sighed, "they're going to put him back on a mental ward. The chief of staff at the hospital here says their ward is sufficient for him and Lindsey Shepard, that psychologist he's been seeing, agrees. They have some fancy terminology for it, but what it comes down to is that he's in some kind of withdrawal and needs to be watched twenty-four hours a day." Then, "I want to *do* something, Sam. But I don't know what."

"I need to find out more about Steve Donovan."

"I'm not sure what you mean."

"If Will didn't kill him, who did?"

"He had enemies. I don't think he was ever faithful to his wife. A man named Thad Owens caught Donovan making out with Thad's wife and he dumped her because of it. I know of at least two times when his wife was going to leave him. And then his business partner and he had a big falling-out."

"That's exactly what I'm talking about. I knew Donovan liked the ladies but I didn't know that his wife had threatened to leave him and I didn't know anything about his business partner."

"But won't Paul be doing the same thing?"

"He's a policeman and he'll go at it his way. But I grew up here. And I have a source he doesn't. Kenny Thibodeau."

"I know this sounds snobbish but I'm so glad he's not a beatnik anymore."

Given the situation, I felt guilty about laughing. "I don't think anybody's been called a 'beatnik' in several years."

"Will always says I'm a square. But you know what I mean about Kenny. He dresses like a normal person and he's married and they have that sweet little girl. It doesn't even bother me that he writes those dirty books anymore. I even bought one at a used-book sale last year. I was embarrassed and the woman who sold it winked at me when I put it in my purse, but I enjoyed it. I thought it would just be filth but it was a really good story and it wasn't all that sexy anyway. Kenny's a good writer."

"And because he writes that column for the newspaper, people tell him things all the time."

"That's another thing I'm happy for him about. He really makes the history of this town interesting."

"And people confide in him because of it. It's weird. They tell him what's going on now, too. So he's a good source."

She leaned back in her chair and stretched her arms out like a comely kitten taking a break. "Umm. This was nice."

"What was?"

"Just now. Talking about what you're going to do. And talking about Kenny. For a little while there I forgot all about where we are and why we're here. I was so far gone I even started thinking about what I was going to make Peggy Ann for lunch. But she's at my sister's until further notice. Right now, for a few days at least, I'm afraid I won't be much of a mother. I'll just sit around and brood."

I'd been distracted by all this, too. All too soon I would need to be in court. While I should have done more prep, I was confident I could handle it. The insurance company would likely settle before the judge appeared. They'd made two offers in the past two weeks but we'd declined them. I was pretty sure this would be an offer we could accept.

"I was just sitting here waiting for you, Sam. I guess I'll go back home now."

As we left the station, she pecked me on the cheek again, squeezed my hand, and then set out for a home without child or husband. Or maybe even future.

5

I got Jamie Newton in trade. When I explain this to people I frequently get a lewd smile, especially after they've seen her.

It happened this way. Her father is an argumentative freelance home repairman who got it in his head that his neighbor had illegally seized a portion of the Newton backyard. He came to me to set up a lawsuit because I have a deserved reputation for taking on cases that others won't, i.e., they don't pay enough. Or, all too often, not at all.

Cam Newton slapped down a hundred-dollar bill on my desk so I said I'd help him. I also said that our chance of winning was slim owing to the fact that the amount of land he wanted ceded back didn't amount to much more than a few yards. He naturally said that didn't matter, that it was the principle of the thing.

Then he told me the real truth, that his

neighbor had insulted Cam's wife one night by smirking that she was a "hefty gal."

We lost the case and Cam lost his money — "lost" as in he couldn't find the other five hundred dollars he owed me. I guess the dealer must have just given him that new Dodge.

He then proposed that his high school-aged daughter would "work off" his debt. I learned quickly not to use that phrase. The smirkers did everything but light up and ring bells the few times I said it.

The fact that Jamie couldn't type, answer phones, operate the Xerox, take dictation, or make tolerable coffee (hers was almost but not quite as bad as mine) didn't make her any less sweet. Though she dressed like the teenage girls on paperback crime novels — tight blouses and skirts, bobby socks and saddle shoes — her naïveté was both endearing and sometimes dangerous.

The latter applied to her choice of boyfriends. Turk was the leader of a local surf band much like the Beach Boys. Since Iowa was a landlocked state, the resemblance to the great Brian Wilson ensemble was strained at best. And as an artist he needed free time with his band for their inevitable — according to him — appearance on *American Bandstand* which would coincide with their album hitting numero uno which would coincide with the launching of their first world tour.

She believed all this and was willing to hand over half her paycheck to support Turk's absolute certain triumph around the world. I knew better than to suggest that she might reconsider Turk as a worthy mate. She got married and got pregnant. Turk was last heard from working in a car wash in Davenport. He'd left after he realized that being married to a sweet, wonderful young woman with a child just got in the way of running Iowa's only surf band.

Motherhood changed her. She managed to complete secretarial courses at a local business college and learned to be an excellent secretary. She even went through the filing cabinets she'd wildly misarranged years ago. Now I didn't have to look for Merle Hennings in F or K or Z. He was right there in H, God love 'im.

Her style in clothes had changed, too. With that freckled country-girl face, so open and pretty, and that body nothing short of a feed sack could hide, she now looked like the kind of secretary you saw in the skyscrapers of Chicago. Very uptown, right down to the newly affected blond pageboy. She can afford this look because one of my clients is the best department store in town. I'm their security adviser. I get a large discount on what I buy there, and so by agreement does Jamie. I also give her a "clothing allowance." Despite the fact that she doesn't feel "ready" to date again, I want her to meet a decent guy who can convince her that not all males are like the vanishing Turk, whose name I never understood because he's black Irish.

She was typing as I walked into my one-room office that rests in the rear of a single-story building that houses in front a Laundromat. Not to worry. The longest any business has lasted up front is eleven months. The Laundromat has been here five months. Somewhere there is a moving van circling and circling and circling, waiting to descend on the Laundromat when it folds. Maybe that XXX bookstore will find a home yet.

"I know Will didn't kill anybody, Sam, even though everybody I talk to says he did. They keep talking about how he was in that mental hospital those times. I had a cousin who was in a mental hospital for about three months a few years ago and she's fine now."

"That's all you have to say is 'mental hospital' and he doesn't stand a chance."

"Some people in this town are narrow-minded."

"It isn't just this town. It's worldwide."

"Really? Everywhere?"

"Just say 'mental hospital' and it doesn't matter if you're speaking Chinese or Spanish, you've convicted the guy."

She just frowned. "Anyway, I've laid everything out for you. For court."

And so she had. About all that was left for me to do was walk to the county courthouse. Then the phone rang and it was for me.

Greg Egan had served in Nam in 1966. For only eight weeks. As a grunt he'd been in some terrible fighting. So terrible that today he was confined to a wheelchair due to the fact that his legs had been surgically removed just below the knees. In some respects he was the conscience of a small group of vets who'd had physical and mental problems in assimilating back home. The wife he'd left behind him when he'd gone to Nam was still behind him. She drove him to the VA three times a week. They were starting the prosthetic process.

"Hi, Sam. I figured you'd know what was going on. All I hear from the news is that Will is a cold-blooded murderer who spent two terms in the bughouse. The murder stuff, that's got to be bullshit, right?"

71

"I'm sure he's innocent, Greg, but there are some extenuating circumstances." I explained the situation as quickly as I could.

"Because that asshole Donovan beat him up? Will is one of the nicest guys I've ever known."

"I agree, but as much as I'd like to, I can't blame the police for making certain assumptions at this point."

"Think if Cliffie was involved." Then, "I know you gotta run. Five of the guys called me in the last fifteen minutes. I said I'd call you and see what was going on. Anything we can do, you know you got it, Sam. I don't have any legs but I've still got a pretty good mind."

I wanted to say you didn't need to say that, Greg, but he was used to people pitying him without quite taking him seriously as a human being. I wondered if Senator O'Shay ever realized things like that.

"I'll keep you posted, Greg."

"Say hi to Karen for us. A very sweet lady."

"She sure is that."

On the walk to the courthouse I didn't think about Will or Karen, I thought about O'Shay. What might have been a political embarrassment for him had been turned into a victory. O'Shay would get to rail again about the "sickness" of the country — and

72

what better example of that sickness than the murder of a brave soldier, a man he'd favored for Congress. Soldiers never "died," they were always "cut down in their prime." Apparently he was unaware that men as old as fifty-five were fighting and dying over there, too.

A press conference was inevitable. He hadn't been scheduled to return to Washington for a few days so he'd likely stage a splashy performance here. If I were one of his aides I would suggest he stage it down in the basement of the funeral parlor where they prepared the corpses for burial. But that would be too much of a reminder about what the good old president Nixon and his de facto vice president Henry Kissinger were really up to, wouldn't it?

Then I started thinking about Will again. I was so tight and angry that I took a pit stop in the john on the second floor of the courthouse. I splashed chilly water on my face and since I was alone — I'd carefully checked — I got down and did twenty push-ups. My max. These gave me a sheen of sweat and for some reason sweating usually relaxed me. I wanted to represent my client as well as I could. I was pretty confident.

I wished I was as confident about Will.

6

In the late 1950s a large number of boys wanted to be James Dean or Elvis or maybe Ricky Nelson. My friend Kenny Thibodeau and I had different aspirations. Kenny wanted to be Jack Kerouac and I wanted to be the actor Robert Ryan.

Kenny did something about his aspirations. If he couldn't *be* Kerouac, he could at least meet him. And so in the summer of 1958 Kenny drove to San Francisco to meet Mr. Kerouac. Kenny spent several days hanging in and around City Lights Bookstore where all the important Beat writers hung out. He did meet the poet Lawrence Ferlinghetti, who also happened to own the bookstore, and he did see, among others, such Beat writers and poets as Gregory Corso and even the famous Allen Ginsberg. But no Kerouac.

A few days before he was to leave, Kenny read some of his poems to some tourists. A man who'd been listening came up to him afterward and offered him a job writing what we'd called at Catholic school "right-handers" (some imagination required here), books with brazenly sexy covers and titles but with almost prudishly written "erotic" scenes inside. Kenny was expected to write one book a month for four hundred dollars.

The man gave Kenny a cardboard box full of what he called his "product" and after shaking hands as Kenny was about to depart said, "Kid, think lesbian."

At the moment Kenny was shoving not one of his monthly paperbacks but a magazine called *Real Man's Adventure* across the table to me.

The mostly naked women with bullwhips had swastikas all over the tatters of their skirts and shirts. A rugged American-hero type was tied to a pole. The lashes had slashed his bare chest mercilessly. "Nazi Gal Killers Made Me Their Sex Slave." I thumbed my way to the contents page to see what pen name he'd slapped on this one. "Burt Scaggs." Manly, very manly.

"Ten cents a word. Eight thousand words — the second lead in the magazine — and I did it in two afternoons. And they want more from me."

I asked what I thought was the logical

question. "If he's their sex slave why are they beating him?"

"They're sadists. All Nazis were sadists."

"Wow, all this and historical accuracy."

He smiled. Kenny had a good novel in him. He'd shown me the part he'd written. I truly believed — and I hoped he did, too — that he would finish the book in a year or so. He was a hell of a good storyteller and a number of his soft-core novels really had strongly developed characters.

We were sitting in the café where the town's lawyers hung out before and after court. I'd won the case for my client. Kenny had agreed to meet me here.

"You know what time it is."

"Yeah, I do."

Melissa Thibodeau was in danger of becoming the most photographed little girl in the state. But she was so damned pretty and sweet, who cared?

The new photographs showed her in her new bonnet and Sunday dress. I did the expected oohing and aahing, but it was *sincere* oohing and aahing. I was Melissa's godfather.

"She's beautiful. Thanks for letting me see them."

I handed them back and then he spoke the mantra. "No way anybody's going to

76

convince me that Will Cullen ever killed anybody."

"I know. That's what most people I've talked to say. But when you put it together as it stands right now you see why Foster thinks he's got a case."

"I hear average citizens call him 'Paul.' "

"Yeah, I don't know about that. It's like a political gimmick. It creates a false sense of security. He's a cop. You can only trust cops so far."

"Wow. You sound like some guys I know who drop too much acid. Mr. Paranoid. Maybe he's just a nice guy." He leaned forward and dragged his billfold out of his right back pocket.

I went through everything again; the kicker was the tire iron.

"Yeah, I see what you mean. But it's not Will. He's just not like that."

"No, he isn't. But I need to move on this. I don't know enough about Donovan to really get going on checking him out. I need to spend time in the library, for one thing. And Karen told me a couple of things. I guess he and his business partner had a falling-out."

"Yeah, big time. Donovan forced him out. Or his new partner did, this Lon Anders."

"That's been proven?"

"Yeah. The old business partner, Al Carmichael, dropped into this depression and finally just said screw it. He let Donovan buy him out for pennies on the dollar. He lives in Pittsburgh now and works for an outfit named ChemLab. I've known Carmichael for a long time. You remember him?"

"Right. Al. He had that cool racing bike when we were in seventh grade. Then he went to public school."

I told him about the angry husband Karen had alluded to.

"Thad Owens. That happened two, three years ago. He caught Donovan and the wife making out at a party. The wife broke down and told him all about her affair with Donovan. He's remarried and could care less about Donovan now. He's got a newborn with the second wife and enjoys himself. I run into him at the supermarket every once in a while."

"Well, I can scratch off those two."

Kenny touched the knot in his tie. Yes, tie. These days instead of looking like the comic beatnik Maynard G. Krebs of the late lamented *Dobie Gillis* show, Kenny affected button-down shirts, chinos, and cordovan penny loafers. His weekly newspaper column gave him some real prominence. There

78

were still people who complained about his books but nonetheless he was asked to talk to groups as respectable as Kiwanis and Rotary. "Don't worry, I've got somebody for you."

"Who?"

"I've heard Anders is as much of a player as Donovan was. And he's a big pilot. Was a fighter in Nam in the mid-sixties and now has his own big-ass plane. I've also been told that lately Donovan and Anders had been arguing pretty violently behind closed doors. But nobody could figure out why. I guess one day Anders came to work with a black eye and wouldn't come out of his office until just about everybody had left that night."

"Then they really weren't getting along."

"I guess Donovan started hanging around his cousin again to the point that some people thought the cousin was a bodyguard. Your old friend Teddy Byrnes."

"You're kidding me. I thought he was still doing time."

"Been out for a month."

Teddy Byrnes had been a member of the Night Devils, a biker gang associated with at least three murders over the years. They'd started after the big war when gangs like them came to prominence. In those days

Marlon Brando in *The Wild One* was their patron saint. But there was a difference between movie violence and real violence. They had escaped punishment for their suspected murders but they had been busted for numerous burglaries, assaults, and armed robberies. Their legend terrified people. Whenever they roared into a park on a sunny Sunday afternoon the picnickers fled.

Teddy Byrnes had been a punk among punks. A pretty-boy psychopath who enjoyed beating people. No guns or knives for him. Just beating them. He'd been in our class for three years but got expelled and went to public school. One beating in particular convinced the county attorney that he had Byrnes nailed, but the victim suddenly declined to testify. Then Byrnes's luck changed. He severely beat a man outside a tavern one rainy night. What he didn't know was that a police officer who'd been checking doors in the downtown area just happened to have turned the near corner and was walking toward Byrnes and his victim. The officer saw everything.

Then Byrnes went looking for a lawyer. . . .

That morning five years ago I'd been prepping for an important case when Jamie said "Oh." There was a disturbed tone in her voice, a mixture of shock and surprise. When I looked up from my papers I saw what that "Oh" was all about. Standing in my doorway was none other than Teddy Byrnes. Jamie had recognized him. A whole lot of people knew who he was. He reveled in it.

He wore a white shirt, blue slacks, carefully tousled hair, and a big black Irisher smile. "They said I should get the best and so here I am, Counselor."

I would have been flattered if I hadn't known the truth. He was out on bail and looking for legal representation. None of the other firms in town would touch him. The public defender he'd had said that he feared for his life. Well-known legal expert Teddy Byrnes hadn't liked the public defender they had come up with and had started shoving him around and making threats.

"No thanks, Byrnes."

But this was a movie moment for him and he played it through. "You know the word I like, Counselor? 'Sumptuous.' I learned that by reading a lot of your friend Thibodeau's books. That surprise you, that bad-ass Teddy Byrnes is a reader? Well I am. I even read Hemingway sometimes. I think you could use that in my defense. That I read a lot.

That I'm not this terrible hood people need to be afraid of." Byrnes was telling the truth. High IQ and a big reader.

"But I forgot what I was talking about. 'Sumptuous.' I see something sumptuous right now." He shifted his gaze to Jamie. She was breathing nervously and staring straight ahead. His legend could do that to you. "I've been to every law firm in town but none of them has got a little gal like you do, Counselor."

The "Counselor" reference had triggered a memory I could not bring into focus. And then it was there. Robert Mitchum in *Cape Fear,* based on one of my favorite novels by John D. MacDonald, whom I'd been reading since sixth grade. Throughout the movie Mitchum mockingly refers to attorney Gregory Peck as "Counselor."

Teddy Byrnes was a movie fan.

Then he did it. Advanced quickly on Jamie. He put his hands on her shoulders and was trying to spin her around in her desk chair so she'd face him fully. She screamed.

I didn't think. I acted.

He was taller, thicker, stronger but I hit him in the side of the face anyway. And in the haze of those few seconds he landed at least six or seven punches on my head and chest and stomach, Jamie screaming all the time.

As he charged out of the office he said: "We'll meet again, you little asshole."

Now, sitting with Kenny. . . .

"Teddy Byrnes," I said.

"Guess he's meaner than ever."

"That's hard to imagine. How he could be meaner."

"I'd be damned careful of him, Sam. Just stick to Lon Anders."

"Yeah," I said. "That sounds like a very good idea. Just sticking to Lon Anders."

My bones still remembered the impact of Byrnes's fists.

7

The Rexall Drugstore was notable in my life for a number of reasons. It was where their metal paperback rack provided a good share of my reading material, which ran to crime fiction of the Gold Medal Books variety. I'd grown up on writers such as Peter Rabe, Charles Williams, Vin Packer and Richard Prather. Not to mention Mickey Spillane. The sandwiches were very good, the coffee was strong and hot, and one of the sweetest, prettiest girls in the entire valley had worked there since we'd graduated from high school. No college for Mary. She had to work to support her father, who was struggling with cancer.

She was always too modest to admit it but people liked to tell her that she looked very much like the actress Jean Simmons, that kind of gentle but riveting beauty. And she did even in the yellow uniform she wore every day.

A man in a suit sitting a couple of stools from me said, "Mary, hon, keep the radio on, will you? I want to hear the senator's press conference."

Knowing my political tastes, she glanced at me and said, "Don't worry, Mr. Costello. It doesn't start for another ten minutes yet."

She brought me coffee black and a small glazed donut. What she didn't bring me was her usual smile and I didn't blame her.

"Hi, Sam. How've you been?"

"Pretty good until last night."

"Poor Will and Karen."

At that Mr. Costello, who owned the haberdashery, snapped, "How about poor Steve Donovan?"

"You're right, Mr. Costello. Of course, poor Steve Donovan. It's just that I don't believe that Will could kill anybody. Sam and I grew up with him."

"I know," Mr. Costello snapped, "in the Hills."

We were both surprised by his anger. Red tinted Mary's lovely face. I said, "Yeah, everybody who grew up in the Hills is a born killer."

"I didn't say that."

"But that's what you meant."

"Drugs, hippies, Negroes wanting everything for free — that's what the Hills has turned into these days. And whether you want to admit it or not, McCain, it wasn't any better in the old days. Now, Mary, turn that radio up so we don't miss anything."

After she turned the volume up, she walked back to me, "The girls leave for three weeks in another week."

"That's right. Wes has them for three weeks." Wes Lindstrom was Mary's ex. His family had owned the Rexall for years but when he'd dumped Mary for the final time — he'd had two trial runs previously — he sold the place and went to live with his new bride in Louisiana. Given his personality, he was probably going to set up a plantation and kidnap him some slaves.

"I've been thinking, Mary —"

Costello was intently trying to listen while intently pretending not to.

"I'll call you later."

"I'd like that, Sam. And so would the girls."

The relationship was just so damned entangled. I had been in love with the beautiful Pamela Forrest from fourth grade until just a few years ago. But she'd never been in love with me. And Mary had been in love with me for just about as long, though I think she really did fall in love with Lindstrom after a few years of going out with him. The complications of all this confused me; I'd always been told by my friends — and my parents — that Mary was the girl I should marry. If it was vanity, as my mom had told me one day long ago, Mary was just as beautiful as Pamela and maybe even more so, and there was no doubt who would make the better wife and mother.

Mary was the sensible choice and since when did reckless buccaneers like Sam McCain settle for "sensible."

So of course I'd told Mary that maybe we should take a little break till I could figure out what was going on. She confused things even more by not reacting with anger or self-pity or even sadness. Just that quiet, dignified Mary acceptance.

"We're interrupting our regularly scheduled program so that we can bring you the following press conference with Senator O'Shay, who is speaking from the steps of the county courthouse."

Senator O'Shay: "This is a sad day not only for me personally but for the entire nation. Our country is in crisis and we need the kind of leadership and patriotism that young men like Steve Donovan can bring to our Congress. But Steve was cut down before he had the chance, cut down by the sickness that infects our nation more and more every day. So before I take questions I want to offer my sincere condolences to Valerie Donovan. The only satisfaction that we can have now is knowing that the person who murdered young Steve will spend his life in prison. Like many of you I would have preferred the death penalty, but the Democrats in our state legislature chose to encourage lawbreakers by doing away with it. Now I'll take questions."

I shook my head and said it loud so Costello would be sure to hear it: "Yeah, if there's one thing O'Shay's known for, it's telling the truth."

I reached over and touched Mary's arm. "Let's get together tonight."

Then I left before I got all that patented O'Shay truth-telling inflicted on me.

8

ZOOM was a motorcycle shop located in the Hills. While they had a few new bikes there they mostly sold very reconditioned ones to the lower-income men and teenagers of the Hills. The owner and chief mechanic was Tim Duffy, who'd done a stretch in Anamosa for stealing cars and selling them to a chop shop in Des Moines. I'd arranged for him to talk to some state bureau boys — name some names — and thus gotten him a sentence reduced to only two and a half years with good behavior. He was now the father of three and an usher at church.

He loved getting greasy. He'd told me that once with a big proud grin, and since he'd been greasy when he told me, I believed him. Today was no exception. T-shirt, jeans, motorcycle boots all glazed with grease as he came walking out of the large garage that sat next to his small showroom and office. He was a country-western fan and so was I if all the songs were sung by Johnny Cash. His mechanics had similar tastes, as you could hear from the twang that bounced off the walls.

"Hey, man, how you doing?"

"Pretty good until last night."

Short, lean with the puggest of noses, he hadn't been cut out for a life of crime. His parole officer told me that he'd never seen anybody turn his life around as absolutely as Duffy had.

"Donovan getting killed. Everybody thinks my friend Will Cullen did it. But I'm sure he didn't."

"Oh, right. That's all anybody's been talking about all morning. Every hour on the hour when the news comes on, my men stop working so they can hear it. It's a pretty big deal, Donovan getting ready to run for Congress and all."

"You ever know Donovan?"

"A little out of my league socially, Sam."

"Yeah, mine, too."

"But I have a feeling I know why you're here. It's because of Teddy Byrnes and him being Donovan's bodyguard."

"A lot of his gang gets their work done here."

"They don't hassle me and I don't hassle them."

"I just wonder if you're picking up anything about Byrnes and Donovan."

"Well, I know that Byrnes was somebody Donovan stayed away from for a long time. I think Donovan tried to help him a couple of times but gave up. And I don't blame him. Byrnes's first stretch was when I was doing mine. Then he did that second one and he just got out. You had to be pretty careful around him. It was obvious he had something wrong with him. Even the real tough guys walked wide of him most of the time. He loved beating on people. I was surprised he got out of there alive."

"I thought he was so tough."

"Yeah, but the other bad guys, man, they're only gonna take so much shit. I think there was something in the wind, in fact, when I was getting out. About taking care of him, I mean. But it never happened, I guess." A laugh. "You know he's a mama's boy, don't you?"

"A mama's boy?"

"Never married, picks up a chick once in a while, but to me it's mostly for appearances. This may not be true but one of the gang told me he sends his mother a card on Valentine's Day. And he's always lived at home. I guess a lot of the prisoners made fun of him behind his back. He had a big photo of his mom on his cell wall while the other guys had girlfriends and wives. Guy he bunked with made a joke about it once and Byrnes broke his arm. Just snapped it in two."

"He's crazier than I thought." Then, "You hear anything about Byrnes and Donovan having a falling-out or anything recently?"

From a back pocket he took a greasy rag and wiped his long, greasy hands on it. Then he took a cigarette from behind his ear and fired it up with a metal lighter that clanked when he flipped the top back. "I haven't heard anything specific but I wondered how long it would last."

"Why's that?"

"With that temper of Byrnes's, he's not one to take orders real well. There was a joke going around in the joint that someday he'd go off and punch out the warden. I never thought it was much of a joke. Byrnes just never took to doing anything except exactly what he wanted to do."

Somebody called him on the loudspeaker. "Be back in a sec."

There was a phone booth on the edge of his property. I went over and called the office.

Three calls: Kenny, Karen, dry cleaning that I hadn't picked up for two weeks. Then

I said, "Jamie, please call the Psychological Partners and see if I can get in to see Lindsey Shepard as soon as possible. I'll call you back when I'm leaving here. I'm at ZOOM right now."

"My daughter loves saying that word. We drove past there one time and she's been saying it ever since."

I gave her the number of the pay phone.

Duffy was waiting for me.

"Sorry to keep you waiting, Tim."

"So what you want is for me to ask around?"

"I'd appreciate it." Kenny Thibodeau was usually the only faux stool pigeon I needed but I didn't think Kenny hung out with too many biker gangs.

"Byrnes takes his bike over to Len Gibbons's shop. He used to go out with Len's sister, only time he ever got sort of interested in a lady. And big surprise — she's still alive. I guess Byrnes loves smacking the gals around."

"One more reason I want him for president." Then, "I'd appreciate any help you can give me."

I pushed my hand out to shake but he held his right hand up and pointed to it with his left. "You don't really want to shake hands with me, now do you, Sam?"

Just then his name was called on the loudspeaker again.

"Thanks, Tim."

"Thanks to you, you mean. You did me a hell of a good turn and I've never been able to pay you back. I'll see what I can find out."

I needed to give Jamie a few more minutes to make her call to Lindsey Shepard. I sat sideways in my car with the door open and smoked. I thought about Mary. I'd always loved her, that was the strange thing. And after the first long-ago time we made love I found her endlessly erotic. But there had been this almost psychotic need for Pamela for so long. . . .

The return call took longer than I'd assumed it would.

"She was in session and the woman who was helping me didn't know if Lindsey was going out for lunch. Lindsey said that if you could come right now she could give you twenty minutes or so."

"Great. Thanks, Jamie."

The name Lindsey Shepard put me in mind of a glacial Grace Kelly blonde but she was instead a winsome little thing who would look young even in her sixties and seventies.

She wore a red blouse with nubby red buttons and a black skirt. She had winsome legs, too, and tiny feet in tiny black flats. Lindsey Shepard, High School Shrink.

She seemed too diminutive for the enormous Victorian house that she and her husband had turned into a fashionable site for both their practice and their living quarters.

"I'm glad to know that Will has you for a friend, Mr. McCain," she said. "But I really can't help you. I guess I'm old-school, but when I was in grad school my favorite instructor always said that one rule was absolute. We aren't to discuss confidential information with anyone unless we feel that a patient is a danger to himself or to someone else."

"You don't consider Will a danger to himself at least?"

"Not enough that I want to talk about him with anyone else."

"Not even the police?"

Her office was a rain forest of heavy plants and an art museum of Chagall and Impressionists. Contradictory styles of art but it worked. From her wide, square window you could see in the distance the limestone cliffs above the river. Peaceful.

"I care about Will, Mr. McCain."

"Sam. Please."

"I care about Will as I do all my patients.

Especially the vets. Very few people seem to appreciate what these young men have been through and the price they've paid. And as for the police, Sam . . . we're social friends with the chief. I guess he expected that I'd pretty much open my files on Will to him but I didn't. He was very disappointed. He even tried to get my husband Randall to help him. Randall saw Will for three months before I did. Then Randall decided that maybe how I approached things might be more productive for Will. But Randall wouldn't help the chief, either. Foster looked angry when he left here earlier."

The smile was pure imp. "Randall tells people we arm-wrestle to see who has the better approach. We actually do argue about it sometimes. My husband has a great sense of humor."

I'd come here hoping she'd give me the kind of information that would buttress the case I was making that Will was an unlikely killer. The only solace I had was that Chief Foster hadn't gotten anywhere, either.

Her phone line buzzed.

"Excuse me a minute." Then, "Oh, sure, Randall. Please do."

After hanging up she said, "Randall would like to stop in and say hello."

I nodded.

Within a minute there was a knock and then a tall, professorial, not unhandsome man with a Vandyke beard and an imposing bearing appeared in the doorway. Both dark hair and beard were streaked with gray. The blue three-piece suit had to be Brooks Brothers. He moved with the ease of a politician comfortable with the meet-and-greet. The hand that clasped mine was firm but not inclined to show off. He was probably eight years or so older than his wife but in very good shape.

"We're very sorry about Will. We know how close you two are. He's talked to both of us about you in sessions. I just wanted to let you know Lindsey and I will do anything we can to help Will and his family without violating our professional ethics."

"I know Karen appreciates that. In fact she appreciates everything you've both done for Will."

"The wives become stress victims themselves," he said. "The man who went overseas is rarely the same man who comes back."

Car horns; a few shouts. Both sounded vulgar on the reticent air of the Victorian house.

Randall Shepard walked over to the window and looked out. "They've been here

97

twice with cameras already. I'm very much a liberal but I can see why people get annoyed with the press. The intrusiveness." He turned back and gave me a smile he'd bought at a store. "People hear this story and they think we're all snake-oil peddlers. It discourages people from coming here. People really do need to come here."

"Randall's right. There are *so* many people we could potentially help. But bad publicity doesn't help."

"Well, right now the only person I'm concerned about is Will," I said.

"Of course," Randall said. "And we feel the same way."

Lindsey checked her watch. "I'm afraid I've got another session in ten minutes." To Randall, "Honey, would you ask Myra to get me something edible from the fridge and get it up here fast?"

"Sure will."

Another handshake.

Then he did one of the damndest things I've ever seen. He gave me a thumbs-up. The beard, the suit, the slight air of stuffiness, the position in the community — I didn't expect it from somebody like him. From Kenny maybe or from one of my clients or from Nick who worked on my car. But not this guy. I wanted him to stay the

98

comfortable stereotype of the somber shrink. You don't want your MD coming in with drinking straws sticking out of his ears.

She was up and moving toward me now, too, as the door closed and Randall went to order her something edible from the fridge. She put her childlike hand in mine and said, "I'm sure this is going to work out all right. I hate all this pop psychology garbage about 'keeping a positive attitude' but I think this is a case where we need to do it. For Will's sake as well as ours."

This was pure rote, nine out of ten of her patients getting it at least once. But ironically I needed to hear it. Sometimes cornball works.

Then she got me to the door in seconds and said to tell Karen to call anytime she wanted or needed to talk.

I left with a full understanding of why both Will and Karen preferred this place to the VA.

9

International Electronics was a handsome white two-story building located in a wooded area that had only started being developed a few years ago. This was the distribution and business center. The factories shipped everything here. By the time he'd been drafted Donovan had steered the company to becoming a major local employer. The company turned out a variety of products, but its mainstay was stereophonic speakers for the very high end — the real audiophiles.

He and his longtime friend Al Carmichael had been music fanatics since grade school, always tampering with record players to get better sounds. As young men they got serious and created speakers that became the standard worldwide.

I hadn't paid much attention to the business over the years but did hear from time to time that their market share was thinning due to both domestic and foreign competition. I do remember that there were layoffs a few years ago. But then there was talk that the company had stabilized and the layoffs had ended. The figure I remembered was that the downturn had cut their work force by about twenty percent.

Even with Donovan gone the business was running full force. The two parking lots were crowded and the loading docks were busy. I parked in Visitors and noticed two special parking spots. One was marked Donovan. One was marked Anders. The latter was filled with a brand-new silver Porsche. I went inside.

Busy in here, too. People with papers hurrying left and right. A long desk where a prim but attractive middle-aged woman sat. She wore a pewter-colored blouse that she filled nicely. A pair of pincenez rested enviably on her bosom. She was so programmed that she couldn't help smiling even on the bereavement watch for her boss.

There was only one way I could make this work. I needed to be brazen. It wasn't my style and a dump truck was pouring vats of acid into my stomach. And the sweat wasn't from the eighty-six-degree heat.

"May I help you?"

"I'd like to see Mr. Anders."

"You do realize what's happened to our founder, don't you?"

"Yes. I'm very sorry. That's why I'm here to speak to Mr. Anders."

"They were not only coworkers. They were best friends. I can't imagine what Lon — Mr. Anders — is going through."

"But he is here. I just saw his car."

She'd admirably kept her irritation in check until now. "May I ask what your name is?"

"Sam McCain."

"And what would your business be with Mr. Anders?"

"Will Cullen is my client. That's what I'd like to see Mr. Anders about."

She leaned most attractively back in her chair and said, "Is this some kind of joke? You represent the man who murdered Mr. Donovan and you want to see Mr. Anders?"

"Afraid that's the case."

She sat up straight again. "Well, I won't let you."

"Of course you will. Your job description includes informing your employers who is here to see them. You don't decide if they see me; that's their decision. Now please inform Mr. Anders that I'm here."

"He's a very good-sized man and he has a very bad temper."

"Then I've been warned and I appreciate it. Now please tell him I'm here." I really liked her perfume. She was probably ten years older than me but that didn't bother me at all.

"You certainly have your gall," she said as she leaned over to finger the proper button. "I'm so very sorry to disturb you, Mr. Anders, but there's a man here who insists on seeing you."

"Who the hell would be bothering me on a day like this? What's his name?"

"He says it's Sam McCain."

There was a considerable pause. "I can't believe this."

"I can't either. I was even considering calling the police and not even telling you."

"Send him in."

"Are you serious?"

"Would I say it if I wasn't serious, Annette? I'm not really in a joking mood today, believe it or not."

"All right." She obviously wanted to ask him if he'd lost his mind. "Thank you, Mr. Anders."

A very nice shape, too, tall and almost regal, her dark skirt loving its duty. I followed in the wake of her perfume.

She opened the door and allowed me to enter what appeared to be a photographic library. Black-and-white as well as color photographs covered half the walls. Each contained dead animals of the kind found in Africa. Rhinos, lions, tigers, even an elephant. And standing with his booted foot on or near their heads was none other than my host, Lon Anders. He wore Hemingway khaki as well as a pith helmet. He'd even grown a wispy beard in some of them. And always at the ready was the rifle he held straight up in his grasp. He'd bravely let his guides find his prey and do everything but kill it for him. They would have made sure that there was no chance the animal would get loose and charge him. And then, heroically, he would blast the shit out of the poor beast.

I thought what I always thought when I saw these great white hunter photographs. We have to start arming the animals. The kind of photo I wanted to see was of a giant elephant's foot on the head of a douchebag white hunter.

The other half of the walls were covered with framed photographs of him in three different types of flight suits during the days he was a pilot in Nam. I thought of Randall Shepard because in one of the pictures he was giving a thumbs-up.

He said, "You've got a lot of balls coming here."

"Your secretary used the word 'gall' instead of 'balls.' "

"Hilarious. Now what the hell do you want?"

"I thought maybe you could help me figure out who really killed Donovan."

"Is this some kind of joke?"

"Your secretary used that line, too."

Lon Anders: running-back size, Scandinavian good looks, Marine Corps blond crew cut and the empty, angry blue eyes I've seen on a number of men convicted of murder. Tan shirt, brown knitted tie, brown pleated slacks. This was the swaggering country club Lothario who tried to get blow jobs from the college-girl waitresses after they were finished for the evening.

"Your nut-job buddy Cullen killed Steve. Talk to Paul Foster, he'll tell you. If Cullen hadn't wigged out he'd probably be signing a confession right now."

"And you were doing what last night?"

He was pretty good. He smiled. He must've had sixty teeth and had elves polish them when he slept at night. "You know, McCain, I've always heard that you were a dumb little jerk but I have to say — you just don't have any common sense at all. If

105

I was worried about being a suspect do you think I'd let you in here?" He pointed to his phone unit. Very sleek. "Why don't you call Paul and tell him you think I killed Steve?"

"You call him 'Paul,' too, huh?"

"Yeah, I call him Paul. We're on a number of committees together. He also likes to play handball. We're friends the same way Steve and I were friends."

"I hear you and Steve weren't good friends at all."

"I'm not even going to comment on that."

"So if you didn't kill him, who do you think did?"

The teeth again. They were spectacular. He went around the desk and sat down. I started to sit in one of the visitor chairs but he said, "Don't even think about it. I don't want your shit-kicker ass contaminating the furniture. This stuff is imported. And you've got three more minutes, by the way, and then I start breaking your bones."

"I hear Teddy Byrnes was playing body-guard for Donovan."

"You have lousy sources if you heard that. Teddy's a cousin of Steve's. He got off to a bad start in life."

My laughter came out much louder than I would have expected. " 'Got off to a bad start in life'? He's a psychopath. What was

Donovan going to do, 'rehabilitate' him?"

"As a matter of fact, in a way he was. One thing about Steve, he always believed in giving people second chances. You should see his office wall. He's got so many plaques from places like Big Brothers you wouldn't believe it."

"I doubt Al Carmichael would agree with that."

He was pretty damned good at scoffing. I wondered if he'd ever done any community theater. "Al Carmichael. He damned near destroyed this company. It took everything Steve and I could do to save it."

"I guess my lousy sources gave me some bad information on that one, too. The way I heard it, you and Donovan screwed him out of his part of the business."

I'd have to look into getting some teeth like that. "It's a good thing you're not a reporter. You'd get your ass sued out of business for slander."

"Libel."

"What the fuck ever. Al Carmichael insisted that we sink money we didn't have into two projects we should never even have considered. But he was adamant. He even threatened to sell his stock to this group that wanted to buy us and then clean out our cash and dump half our employees and then sell us for a big profit. I guess your lousy sources didn't tell you anything about that, did they?"

I have the bad habit of wondering how people I meet would do as lawyers. He would work well either way, defense or prosecution. He could lie *without* his pants catching fire.

"Seems to me if Donovan was really your friend, you'd want to help me find out who really killed him."

"Right. And Lee Harvey Oswald didn't really kill President Kennedy."

"I wasn't a big fan of Donovan's," I said quietly. "But he deserved better friends than you."

The teeth again. He started to say something, then shook his head.

He said nothing more to me and neither did the sumptuous Annette as I walked out the front door.

10

Jamie said, "I don't know how they're going to put a parade together on such short notice."

"O'Shay's so desperate to get reelected I'm sure he'll find a way."

"My mom always votes for him. I think it's his hair. He reminds her of some old-time actor I've never heard of. I don't like him because of what he said about Negroes one time. I had three Negro girls in my homeroom and there were a lot of people who were terrible to them. It used to make me so mad. So Senator O'Shay goes ahead and says that too many of them would rather live on the dole than work. Our pastor gave a sermon about people who talk that way. You could tell he was pretty mad. He even used Senator O'Shay's name. But somebody in the church must have written him and told him what the pastor said because he wrote the pastor a letter and said he wanted it read to the whole congregation."

O'Shay was spending time addressing a church whose pastor he'd pissed off? Not exactly a good use of his time.

"Did he read it?"

"He did, yes, but then he attacked Senator O'Shay again for things that were in the letter." A happy look. "Most of us were so proud of Pastor Jim."

I was waiting on a call to Al Carmichael at ChemLab in Pittsburgh. Who better to talk about Steve Donovan and Lon Anders than their former business partner? Good reporters always use disgruntled sources. Not all of them are reliable but the ones who are can give you explosive information and insights.

Meanwhile I called the hospital and asked for the psych ward. The nurse I talked to sounded wary and weary. "All calls about Mr. Cullen go through our public relations office downstairs. If you'd told the receptionist what you were after she would've directed you there."

"All I want to know is if his condition has changed."

A put-upon sigh. "No, it hasn't."

"Thank you."

By the time I got "Thank" out she'd hung up.

"A man named Al Carmichael is on the phone for you," Jamie said after the phone rang next.

"Thanks for returning my call, Al."

"I'm assuming this has something to do with Steve Donovan's death. I still have friends back in Black River Falls and three of them have called me about it. I think they half expected me to jump up and down and celebrate, but as much as I hated him at the end we'd been good friends for four or five years and so I have good memories of him, too. So if you want some kind of bad quote about him, I'm not going to give it."

"Would the same apply to Lon Anders?"

A snort. "Exactly what are you looking for, Sam?"

I told him. I also explained that I did not believe that my friend Will Cullen had killed the man. And that I was serving as both his lawyer and his investigator.

"You think that's smart? It's pretty hard to be objective in a case like this."

"I've known Will all my life. I trust my instincts."

"Well, it's your call, Sam."

"So how about Lon Anders?"

"A total piece of shit. As soon as Steve

hooked up with him things started to change at the place."

"How so?"

"Somehow Anders was able to convince Steve that he knew something about our business. Anders is a quick study, I'll give him that, but he's basically a peddler. He liked to give pep talks to all the workers there. They thought he was an arrogant, stupid blowhard and they were right. After he got Steve's ear, my staff and I could never get Steve to prototype anything we came up with. And we knew why. It was a turf battle. And what Steve never realized was that Anders would someday push him aside just as he'd pushed me aside. Three of my best staffers quit. They were so frustrated they couldn't take it anymore. Anders took it on himself to find their replacements. They knew even less about our business than Anders did. But behind my back they reported everything to him. What he was doing was building a case against me for Steve's sake. I have a family history of depression. And that's what landed on me. Anders was nice enough to spread the word that I had 'mental problems' so people started looking at me as if I'd bring a shotgun to work and kill two or three of them. So finally I just resigned and let Steve buy me out for pennies. But I just wanted out of there and didn't really care what he paid me."

My mind fixed on him talking about Anders someday pushing Donovan aside.

"What were profits like when you left?"

"I admit to being petty when it comes to Anders and the clowns he'd hired. But the products they came up with made money. I couldn't believe it but I saw it on the P&L sheets and there wasn't much I could say about it."

"Have you had any contact with Donovan since then?"

"No. I didn't know what I'd say to him or what he'd say to me. But today . . . well I think maybe I should have called him once in a while."

"This has been very helpful, Al."

"I don't really see how, but if you say so, I'm glad."

"Thanks," I said. And I meant it.

I was excited about it.

One of the experiences I've never had as an investigator is being followed. The police do it all the time in unmarked cars and it is one of the staples for most private investigators. But it had never happened to me. And in comic strips, short stories, novels, TV shows, and movies, private investigators do it — and have it done to *them* — all the time.

So I was sort of enjoying it.

He'd followed me at about a half-block distance from my office. Drab four-year-old Dodge sedan.

I had half a tank of gas so I was able to run him for half an hour, even up into the limestone cliffs above the river. He was good, very good. Easy peasy. Never panicked once. Just stayed behind me and never once came close to losing me.

After a while it got boring. Plus I was hungry. My exhaustion needed to be fed.

I drove to a Mexican restaurant called "Carlos'." He was smart. Seeing where I was going he pulled into a parking space across the street and waited till I went inside. I was pretty sure he had no idea that I'd finally spotted him.

From my booth I could see him. An older man a little slumped in the driver's seat. He'd occasionally glance over at me and I'd glance away. Eye tag.

I had a taco and a glass of Pepsi. The Pepsi was warmer than the taco. I'd have to remember not to come in here again.

After relieving myself in the john, I walked through the kitchen and out the back door.

Numerous pairs of eyes watched me. One man said, "Hey." But I didn't wait to find out if that was a friendly "Hey" or an unfriendly one.

There was an alley across the street. There would be no way he could see me from where he was parked.

The old battered garages in this poor neighborhood reminded me of my boyhood in the Hills. Everything there had been in a perpetual state of rot and falling-down, too, but alleys and half-collapsed garages had been a fine place to sail the imaginary seas you saw in all those Technicolor pirate movies or to hide behind huge pretend boulders to shoot at bad guys who populated all the B Western movies.

I came out a block behind him. The temperature had to be approaching ninety because even this slight bit of exercise soaked my shirt. He wouldn't be having that problem. Even at four years of age his car probably had air conditioning.

I had had to cross a street, which gave him the opportunity to see me. Now I walked up the sidewalk leading to his car, which gave him another opportunity. From what I could tell he didn't ever glance in his rearview or look around.

I opened the passenger-side door before

he could do anything about it. But then he didn't *have* to do anything about it because he was holding a Smith & Wesson Model 586 with the four-inch barrel pointed directly at me. He had one of those old-time smooth radio voices that suggested both manliness and more than a hint of irony.

"That looked like a terrible place to eat, McCain." But before I could say anything, he said, "It's too hot to keep the door open. Get in and sit down. And if you're with weapon, please put it in my glove compartment."

With weapon. Despite the situation I liked that.

"No weapon."

"Good."

I sat.

He resembled the actor Robert Montgomery. Intelligent, slightly slick manliness. Gray-streaked hair combed straight back; the blue gaze probably not as strong as he would have liked. Still looked good in the somewhat worn three-piece suit.

Now that I could see him close-up the fine features and baritone voice were all that was left of a man who had, most likely, seen better days. The right arm was dead, just hung there. And as I watched him he convulsed almost imperceptibly. Even so, in snapshot he looked like all the upscale private investigators on the covers of the used mystery pulps I used to buy for three cents apiece.

"Stroke."

"I'm sorry. And I'd be even sorrier if you weren't pointing that at me."

"My apologies. I never liked it when somebody pointed a gun at me, either." He set the gun on his lap.

Then we just sat and looked at each other for a minute.

"We're doing the same thing, McCain."

"Yeah, and what would that be?" But I had a pretty good idea.

"You haven't figured it out by now?"

"You're a private investigator."

"That's right."

And then — the air of dash, the sleek patter, the stroke — I recognized who he really was.

"You're Gordon Niven."

"At your service. And in case you're wondering how I can still get work, I do it all by phone and mail. I sound pretty sturdy on the phone. They call me and tell me their problem and I agree to help them on my own terms. Not everyone agrees but at least thirty or forty percent do."

In Des Moines there was this legendary

investigator named Gordon Niven. He'd been a bona fide spy in the big war and the highest-priced private investigator in Chicago for the fifteen years following it. Then he fell in love with the wife of a prominent radio host. She left her carousing and abusive husband on the condition that they settle in Des Moines, her hometown. His work crisscrossed the state. He broke up counterfeiting rings, drug rings, seditionist rings and did every other kind of investigative work as well. He built and lived on a giant sprawl of an estate and never quite quit courting his new wife. I'd read his interviews in the paper. Despite his usually polished demeanor he still got downright corny about her. But I thought I'd heard a rumor that they'd split up.

"You mind if I ask why you're following me?"

"I need some help." He clapped his dead arm. "There's this and there's the fact that you may be the man who'll help me finish up what I'm doing here and get back home. My wife and I have reconciled. I miss her. And frankly, I'm tired."

"Maybe I could be of more help if you told me what's going on."

"That would violate the private-eye code."

"What private-eye code?"

118

"Haven't you ever read your Raymond Chandler?"

"Of course."

"Well, Marlowe adheres to a strict moral code. In fact Marlowe is why I got into this business after the war. Spying's a very dirty game. I had to kill two people and let someone I liked be tortured to death. No moral code in spying. The opposite, if anything. Then I happened to read *Farewell, My Lovely* and as ridiculous as it sounds I realized that that was a field where I could make my own moral code and not be forced to violate it."

Here I was sitting with a living legend who was telling me that he partially became a living legend because of Philip Marlowe.

"So when do I get to know what's going on?"

With his good hand he waved me off. "Go somewhere interesting, will you, McCain? So far this has been pretty boring." The grin made it clear he was kidding me.

"I'll do what I can for you, your Lord and Majesty."

"You have to admit, you're at least a little bit pleased to be working with me."

I sure as hell wasn't going to give him the satisfaction of agreeing with him.

"Take care of yourself, McCain. I'm relying on you."

I got out of the car and started walking to the rear of it when I looked through the backseat window and saw three manila file folders spread across it. The folders didn't interest me but the black-and-white photograph of the woman lying on one of them did.

Her image stayed with me all the way back to my car.

What the hell was Gordon Niven doing with a photo of Steve Donovan's wife Valerie?

PART TWO

"Our numbers have increased in Vietnam because the aggression of others has increased in Vietnam. There is not, and there will not be, a mindless escalation."
— Lyndon B. Johnson

11

Jamie was just telling me that Chief Foster had called wanting to talk to me when Foster himself walked through the doorway and said, "I was headed to the courthouse but when I saw your car I thought I'd stop in."

In order to see my car Foster would have to pull into an alley and check the space allotted for three cars. Not quite as casual as he made it sound.

"Think I could get a few minutes of your time?"

"Sure."

He glanced at the back of Jamie's head. "Kind of stuffy in here. How about we go sit on the steps."

"Who wants to be in air conditioning when you can soak in the ninety-degree temperature?"

"I couldn't have said it better myself."

I went down the hall and dragged a couple

of Pepsis out of the vending machine and then followed him out the door. Nothing more comfortable than concrete steps.

"You want to go first, Sam?"

"Oh, the working together thing."

"You have the edge. You know this town a lot better than I do."

"Well, one thing I've found out is that I think Lon Anders and Steve Donovan may have had a falling-out over business."

"And why would you think that?"

"I talked to Donovan's old business partner. He said that Anders wanted the business all to himself. That being the case, maybe Anders killed Donovan."

Two kids with Dracula T-shirts came strolling down the alley toward us. I'd seen them many times before. They liked to sit on a nearby deserted loading platform and smoke cigarettes. Foster's black hard-ass Mercury with its whip antenna said police. The kids glared at us as they passed by. They had squatters' rights on the loading platform. This was summer vacation. Kids were supposed to do what they wanted with no adult interference.

"Guess I'd need some more evidence than that. The way Anders tells it, Carmichael almost ruined the company."

"Then there's a guy named Teddy

Byrnes."

"Donovan's cousin?"

"Uh-huh."

"Why would Byrnes kill his meal ticket?"

"Because he's insane. Maybe Donovan pissed him off. You don't piss off Teddy Byrnes."

Then it was his turn. He was so laid back he probably didn't need Valium for his colonoscopy. No problem, man. Just shove it right in there. I'm fine.

Everything he'd learned pointed to Will being the killer. He'd interviewed Anders ("By the way, he told me that he'd like to set you on fire and then drown you; I have to admit that the boy has a temper.") and Anders was home from seven o'clock to six thirty this morning when he woke up. His lady friend would testify to that. "That isn't necessarily a great alibi but nobody seems to have seen him in or around the crime scene. And believe me, with that car of his just about everybody would've noticed him."

"Maybe he drove a different car."

"Maybe. But the difference between Anders and Cullen is that people *can* place Cullen at the crime scene. And then there's the matter of motive. Donovan had humiliated him."

"Cullen went looking for him to make things right. To apologize."

The pipe came out again. He filled it, tamped it, lighted it. Some men look so damned comfortable with themselves when they smoke their pipes. Cigarettes are for nervous, uptight people. Like me most of the time.

"And there he sits, Sam. He can't help me and he can't help you. And he can't help himself. He just sits there or lies there and he's beyond reaching."

The pipe smoke was almost exhilarating. I wanted to run right down to the tobacco shop and buy myself one. A good one. One that would make me look serious and contemplative. People whispering behind your back, "That little bastard is a genius."

"So you're fixated on Will."

"Sam, give me somebody else to be fixated on and I'll jump right across."

I slapped a mosquito with so much force against my cheek that I could feel pain in my forehead. A mistake. I didn't want one of those military hospital headaches.

"Bring me what I need and Will's a free man."

"You don't really believe he's guilty, do you?"

"Now you don't really think I'd give you

an honest opinion on that, do you? I'm not very bright but I'm not dumb enough to say that to his lawyer. We go to trial and you put me on the stand and make me say that I told you I didn't think he was guilty —"

"Then you do think he's innocent."

"He could be but right now I'd have to say that he looks guilty. I keep telling you to look at the evidence. You keep denying any possibility that he's guilty. But if you could be even a bit objective —"

"I think I can be. I think I am."

"Well, I hope for your sake you're right. Because otherwise I'm afraid you're wasting your time."

And with that he stood up with his pipe and his skeptical police eye and reached out and offered me his hand.

"If you come up with something new —"

"I'll let you know." I almost said "Paul" but I was not going to give in to that.

I watched him walk to his car and then we exchanged a wave and I went back inside to the civilizing effects of air conditioning.

Kate was the star. You couldn't not watch her. She was four and dressed in a blue sweatshirt with a cartoon cat on it. Presumably the cat was from a Saturday morning show sponsored by one cereal or another.

129

She was possessed of amused blue eyes and blond hair that looked so soft it would probably disintegrate if you touched it.

Nicole was five and intensely serious. Her dark hair and dark eyes were almost perfect matches for her mother's. Every once in a while as we ate she would fix her eyes on the wonderfully childish Kate with a disdain befitting royalty.

Maybe it was because of the green linen tablecloth and all the darker green dishes and coffee cups and cloth napkins that I had second helpings of roast beef and mashed potatoes. It had been quite a while since I'd had a family meal.

Then as the sky in the dining room windows turned into violet night, Mary announced that it was time for the girls to take their baths and get ready for bed.

I got kisses from both the girls. Kate's was earnest and a little sloppy. Nicole's was dry and quick.

And just then I realized that in her quiet and proper way there was something like sorrow in those dark eyes of hers. And then I thought — I catch on quick — of what she'd been through with her parents these past few years. The rancor and anger. Maybe Kate wasn't old enough yet to completely understand what was happening. Certainly she would have understood the rage of both parents. That would have been terrifying. But Nicole was old enough — and certainly bright enough — to know the implications of all the torment. Her father would never live with them again. The people who had comprised her family would never be her family again. I gave her a hug.

Kate said she wanted to show me her cat drawing but Mary said some other time. "Kate's a genius at thinking up reasons not to take her bath."

Then she hustled them off with Kate throwing " 'Night" over her shoulder.

After Mary came back, I said, "You remember that job I had in high school washing dishes over at Romano's Pizza?"

"You're going to tell me that you miss washing dishes."

"Not washing them, drying them."

"I see. Well, I'm certainly not going to stop you."

For the first five minutes in the kitchen we made out. My hands were all over her and she was all over me.

Then Kate called out for her and we had to give up those ferocious high school sex moments.

When she came back she said, "Kate

couldn't find her walrus."

"That sounds bad."

"We were at the dime store one day and she saw this cheap little stuffed walrus and begged me to buy it for her. She was two. It's like some kind of lucky charm or something. Somehow it had fallen behind her bed. I got it for her and she gave me one of those hugs you can never forget."

"You're a good mother."

"I could be a lot better, believe me."

"Oh, right, I forgot what a terrible woman you really are."

"You've always kind of idealized me, Sam. I've always wanted to say that to you but the right time never came around. This is the right time. You boys in high school and college always said 'She's the kind of girl you marry' or something like that. I think that's how you've always thought of me. I don't literally mean marrying me but that I was the 'good' girl or something like that and Pamela was the bad one. But Pamela wasn't bad; she was just confused about her real feelings. And I wasn't all good, either. I lost my virginity when I was sixteen. I lied because I knew you'd lose respect for me if I didn't."

Well, there you go. She'd told me that I was the first lover she'd ever had. And that was when we were out of high school.

This was the seventies. I indulged in liquor, grass and sex. I'd lost my religious faith, I'd lost most of my faith in the political system and I knew how corrupt our system of justice was. And if I had to sit down and count up the number of lies I'd told in my life, a fair share to women I'd cared about, I would be one hundred and thirty-four before I could stand up again.

But this hurt me, what she said.

"I'm sorry I lied to you, Sam."

"Oh, that's all right."

"Sam, I'm standing right here and I can *see* that it's not all right. I lied and I'm sorry. And it was only once and the next time I slept with anybody it was you."

I proudly kept a book on feminism on my coffee table to show the young ladies I tried to charm that I was no Cro-Magnon macho moron. But here I was trapped in that old virgin trap. I'd always thought I was the first with Mary.

"Slap me."

"What?"

"Slap me."

"Sam, are you all right?"

"No, I'm not all right. I'm thinking like morons think."

"And how would that be?"

"I don't want to say. That's why I want you to slap me. Bring me to my senses."

"Either you're mad at me for lying to you or you're mad at me because you weren't the first."

"The first."

"The lying?"

"Uh-huh."

"I don't blame you."

"And a little because of the second."

"Because I wasn't a virgin when we finally slept together?"

"Yeah, a little bit of that."

"Sam, please don't be like my brother."

"Stan?"

"Yes."

"What about him?"

"He has this wonderful girlfriend. And she really is wonderful. And he loves her. I've never seen him like this, but he won't marry her."

"Because she's not a virgin?"

"Exactly."

"He lost his virginity when he was fourteen."

"He told *you* that, Sam?"

"No, my dad caught him in the back of his old panel truck."

"God, I can't believe how he's been about this whole thing. About not being able to marry her. This is the seventies. Girls have as much right to have sex as boys. I know how it's killing him. One night he started crying about it. I just held him the way I did when he was little and he got hurt or somebody had said something mean to him. He'd never admit it but he's pretty sensitive. And then it wasn't funny or even ridiculous anymore because I could see it was tearing him apart. How much he loved her and wanted to marry her but couldn't because of this stupid idea he had in his head."

"So is he ever going to marry her?"

"October fifth."

"Seriously?"

"Seriously. He finally came to his senses."

I took her arms and pulled her to me. Good Mary, bad Pamela. All good uncomplicated Mary and bad complicated Pamela. Reliable Mary and exciting Pamela.

But just as I was about to kiss this brand-new Mary, she stopped me. "One more thing, Sam. I know you think I kind of hover around you too much and I probably do. But you are sort of needy and that brings it out in me."

"I'm needy?" My voice went up an octave.

"Sorta, sometimes, you know in little ways. But that's part of why I love you.

You've helped me so many times, too. I'm just as needy as you are."

Anger flushed my face — I could feel it — and then without realizing it I started laughing. "You weren't a virgin and you lied about it and now I'm 'needy'? Whatever happened to that perfect little Mary I knew?"

"I'm right here, the real Mary, Sam. That other one was just in your imagination. And part of that was my fault, with the lie and all. But please, Sam, I don't want to be 'good Mary' anymore. All right?"

Bad Mary was great.

If you couldn't get laid in 1971, you couldn't get laid at all.

This was according to just about every magazine, newspaper, and newscast you consulted for information on how the luckier half was living.

This was the era of free love, though that phrase had faded.

In the big cities they had sex clubs. You went in and had sex in your choice of many rooms. Sometimes you went alone and sometimes you brought your spouse. You could have sex by twos, threes, fours and just about any other number you wanted. And this was hetero sex or gay sex.

Swinging was also big. Suburban neighborhoods became the site of serious orgies. Marriages broke up, venereal disease ramped higher, and one prominent bestselling shrink said that if you wanted to have an affair it was none of your spouse's business. The thing was to please yourself. It took a while before someone pointed out that this was what you might call — if you wanted to hurt the shrink's feelings, the dear — sociopathic.

In Black River Falls we had one dance club/singles bar and that was The Retreat. A standard-issue bar had been gutted, a sparkling ball had been mounted on the ceiling, and a dance floor had been built. There was even a long mahogany bar perfect for leaning against if you thought you were cool enough for that particular pose.

Singles rejoiced and were still filling the place. The hopeless were soon banished by shunning. If you were too old, too nerdy, too unfashionably dressed, too dull by reputation, or too feckless with pickup lines — out.

What you have to understand here is that most of the popular people at The Retreat had been the popular ones in school. So what you had were the cheerleaders, the sports stars, the rich kids, the prom queens, and the just plain good-lookers of the past ten years from the town's two high schools.

In other words, you were back in tenth grade when you didn't get invited to any of the really groovy parties.

I never went there often enough to get shunned. I had dates from time to time who insisted we go but I always managed to get us gone early.

Tonight I was here on assignment.

The Retreat was crowded. That sparkling, revolving dance ball limned the heads and shoulders of all the dancers while other couples sat in shadow groping each other.

Cathy Vance sat at the bar sideways, her long, slim legs almost as enticing as that wild mane of dark hair and that vivid theatrical face of hers. She was always number one or two on the who'dya like to fuck list in high school. Tonight she treated us to a silver summer blouse and a skirt that could break your heart.

I was surprised that there were only two guys putting the moves on her. I stood to her left so eventually she'd have to see me. When she did, she said, "Who let you in, McCain?"

Her would-be suitors — all unbuttoned shirts and bell-bottomed plaid trousers — glared at me. The yellow-haired one said —

actually said — "You want him gone, babe?"

Even as a little girl her smile had been wan, even sad.

"No, I'm going to give him a few minutes and if he tries to stay longer then I'll want him gone."

"You got it, babe," said the dark-haired one.

They gave me their best TV bad-guy stares, then moved down the bar.

"Hey, babe," I said.

"Go fuck yourself, McCain."

"One of them could be husband number three if I'm not mistaken?"

She waved her empty glass at the bartender. "I'm worried about Will. I still care about him."

"That's why I'm here. I'm wondering if you care about him so much that you send him threatening letters in the mail."

"Does that sound like something I'd do?"

With a fresh drink in her hand, she said, "He didn't kill Steve Donovan."

"You didn't answer my question."

"Yes, I did. I asked you if that sounded like me."

For all her audacious sexuality the one man she'd loved had deserted and humiliated her. She and Will had gone together through most of college but the summer he met Karen he dropped her with no warning. Two marriages and numerous men later, she'd never recovered.

"I think you were sleeping with him again."

"I don't do married men."

"And you don't send threatening letters in the mail."

Their official relationship had ended many years ago. Will told me over the years that she'd sent birthday cards and Christmas cards to him at his veterinary clinic. Her interest in him had never waned. What if they'd had an affair and then he'd ended it again? What if she saw an opportunity to punish him by killing Donovan and letting Will be blamed?

"Somebody made it look as if Will killed Donovan. You knew Donovan, didn't you?"

"Now and then." Coy. I hate coy.

"I thought you didn't do married men."

"There are exceptions to every rule." Still coy but then angry. "I'm sick of talking about this. I don't appreciate you hounding me when I'm trying to relax. You always were a pain in the ass, McCain."

"You going to sic your boyfriends on me?"

"I will unless you walk out of here right now."

"I'm pretty sure you had an affair with

him and I'm pretty sure you mailed him those things."

"You sound desperate, McCain. Now leave me alone."

A single glance from her started the boyfriends walking toward me. Fists at their sides.

"This isn't over, Cathy. Believe me."

Then I made myself gone.

12

"Do you think Count Chocula is real?" Kate asked me with professorial seriousness while she was eating some. I'd dropped by for breakfast.

If there was an Olympic event for eye-rolling, Nicole would win outright.

"Well, some say he's real and some say he's not," I said.

"Now, there's a politician," Mary laughed.

"Of course he's not real." Nicole would also win the Gold for scoffing.

"But we saw him in that movie."

"That was an actor playing him, sweetie."

She eyed her sister with grumpy spite. "Well, I can believe in him if I want."

As breakfast went on I had the same conflicted feelings I'd had the night before. Family life was enjoyable and comforting; family life was confining. Mary came as part of a package deal.

"Can we go to the parade now, Mommy?"

Kate said.

"It'll be a little while, honey."

"I want to be in the band when I'm old enough," Nicole said. "The uniforms are cool."

"Her music teacher said that she's really got talent," Mary said. "Right now she plays the piano. This coming school year she'll be part of a recital."

"I want to play in a band and be a rock star."

"Somehow, Kate, that doesn't surprise me."

She blessed me with one of her baby smiles.

I was just thinking about repairing to the john — the house was nice enough to have three, believe it or not; main floor, second floor, and basement (pot and shower), perfect for a new man of the house — when the phone rang.

There was a yellow extension phone on the kitchen wall. The table where we ate put me closest to it so I jumped up and got it.

"We're trying to reach Mr. Sam McCain." A serious-sounding woman.

"This is he."

"This is St. Mark's hospital. A man named Gordon Niven listed you as next of kin."

"He did?" The shock in my voice alerted

Mary. She'd been interested in somebody calling me here but now she was even more interested because of my tone. "I'm not really his kin."

"Well, he listed you, Mr. McCain. You do know him, don't you?"

"Yeah. I guess. Slightly, I mean."

"I have to admit this is strange. We were going to call his residence in Des Moines — that's where his driver's license says he lives — but in his wallet he put a card that reads: In case of emergency call Sam McCain. We tried your home phone and there was no answer. A woman here knows Mary and said to try you at her number."

"What's wrong with him?"

"He was severely beaten sometime last night. He was found this morning in a parking lot adjacent to the Royale Hotel, which is where he was registered. We checked. Whoever beat him jammed him behind a dumpster. He has a concussion, two broken ribs, and a broken jaw. He can't talk because his jaw is wired shut. Right now he's sleeping. Do you know anything about the incident?"

"Not right now. You're aware that he's a private investigator? He's in town because of a case. I'd like to see him as soon as I can."

"My guess is that it will be much later in the day and maybe not even then. You'll just have to call and check on his condition. He's understandably exhausted and very weak."

"Yes, of course. Well, I'll check later today. Thanks for calling."

"Thank you for your help, Mr. McCain."

The girls had skittered off. Mary had watched and listened to me with the fervor she brought to her soap operas. Even in high school she was known as the soap queen.

"That sounded ominous," she said as I sat down.

"It is." I explained to her who Niven was. "I suppose Foster has already tried to interview him. I hope he didn't have any luck. Niven might not be able to talk but maybe he could write things down."

"I thought you liked Foster."

"Pretty much I do. But I'm not sure he'll be making the connections I am. I saw a photo of Valerie Donovan in Niven's back seat with some file folders. I'm assuming he's been hired to investigate her."

"Investigate her for what?"

"I'm not sure yet. But Foster needs proof that Will didn't kill her husband. So I have to come up with some believable alternative to what Foster believes happened. I'd

145

planned on visiting Niven's hotel room when he was out."

"That has to be illegal."

"It is. But even if he caught me he wouldn't call Foster because that would get Foster interested in *him*. And Niven likes glory. He wouldn't want to share it with a cop."

"Do you like Niven?"

I told her about the image I'd had of him — the legend — and how he turned out to be. "There's an old Hollywood saying, 'Never meet your heroes.' You know, because you'll be disappointed in some way. And that sure was true about meeting him. But there's something sort of sad about him, too. He's just sort of this dumpy guy who obviously has a great brain for this business."

She touched her napkin to her perfect lips. "Well, I need to get the girls ready for the parade. It starts at nine thirty. I don't suppose you're going."

"I doubt I'll have time. I'm going to Niven's hotel. I want to check on some things."

She came over to me and tilted my head up and kissed me with erotic tenderness on my mouth. "Needless to say, I had a great time last night."

"Needless to say, I did, too."

"The girls really like you. Especially Kate."

"She's better than any show on the tube."

Then I pulled her to me and pushed the side of my head into her breasts. She laid her hand on the side of my head and embraced me even tighter.

We stayed exactly like that until Kate ran in and said, "Mommy, can I wear my red socks? Nicole says my yellow ones'd look better."

Home life; home life.

The Royale boasts that such presidents as Herbert Hoover, FDR, Harry Truman, and Dwight Eisenhower all stayed there when they came here to campaign. True enough, but there was no alternative. The somewhat artistic but talentless son of a hotel magnate thought he'd show the old man how he could duplicate a New York or Chicago hotel right here in Iowa. He had impregnated a freshman girl at the university and wanted to be near her.

You want splendor, he gave you splendor, right down to the giant sculpture of a giant male archangel swooping up a female archangel right in the lobby. Neither happened to be clothed. You want classical music, he gave you classical music by busing in musicians from Iowa City four nights a week. You want gourmet dining, he gave you chefs from the major American cities and one from Paris. Their cuisine was fine but I always wondered how the locals took to it.

In 1952, after being spurned by his third wife, the somewhat artistic son of the magnate hurled himself off the sixth-floor veranda of his hotel apartment. The magnate took over the hotel, stripped it of its too, too finery and ran it, for the first time, at a profit.

This morning I walked into the lobby with two tens and two twenties in my pocket. I went immediately to the head bellboy. He had a very bald head, a rangy body, and eyes that appeared to have knowledge of every sin ever committed by mankind. His nametag, hanging on the breast pocket of his blue-and-white uniform, read: CHARLES.

"Help you, sir?"

"You didn't happen to work last night, by any chance?"

We stood to one side of the main desk. Two female clerks in blazers were saying how much they'd wanted to watch the parade, which was starting in less than an hour.

Charles said, "Yesterday was my long day. I worked until about eleven last night."

"You see anything odd going on? Maybe somebody who looked like he might be trouble?"

"Well, I saw the guy who had some drinks with Mr. Niven in the bar. If that's what you're wondering about."

"What time was this?"

"Later on. Nine thirtyish. He didn't look right to me."

"I'm not sure what you mean."

"The way he looked. A lot of our traffic is salespeople. We have a nice-sized ballroom for small conventions. You know the kind of people I'm talking about. Suits, ties, suitcases, briefcases. Business guys. This guy — six-two, maybe up to six-four. Tan suede suit coat which is two hundred a pop easy. Brown sports shirt under it. Brown slacks. West Coast kinda look, if you know what I mean. And he walks in and the look he gives me. I'm a piece of shit. You ever get a look like that?"

"Maybe once or twice." Or three or four hundred times.

"He walks like he's gonna attack somebody."

"Lot of black curly hair?"

"How'dya guess?"

"Lucky, I guess. So then what happened?"

"He goes in the bar and maybe an hour

later he comes out with Niven. They walk over to the elevator and that's the last I see of them."

"You remember Niven's room number?"

"Three twenty-six."

I gave him one of the tens.

I rode to the third floor with a pair of older salesmen who were blaming the decline in their business on hippies. From what I could tell they sold shoes wholesale.

"They don't even take baths that often. Why are they going to give a shit about shoes that really support their feet?"

"I just wish I was getting as much sex as those bastards get."

"I just wish they were wearing out shoes when they were getting it."

When the doors opened to the third floor a man smiled at me and I smiled at him. It was Chief You-Can-Call-Me-Paul Foster.

As soon as the doors closed behind me, he said, "Let me see if my psychic powers are working today. You're here to check out the room of a man named Niven. I believe the first name is Gordon."

"A legend in my business."

"Would that business be lawyer or investigator?"

"I'm sure you already know the answer to that."

"The hospital tells me that he'd suffered a stroke a while back. This sure as hell couldn't be any good for him."

"He's a nice guy. And I wasn't exaggerating about him being a legend."

"I see. I'm told that Mr. Niven has been in town for two days. I assume you ran into him?"

"Excuse me." A man approached, checking his watch, his sweaty face suggesting that he'd overslept. He moved us aside and then practically dove onto the elevator when it opened up.

After the doors closed again, I said, "Yeah, I did run into him."

"A prominent private investigator comes to our little community at the same time one of our most prominent citizens is murdered. Am I wrong in seeing a possible connection?"

"He was here before Donovan was murdered."

Then he struck. "You really piss me off." The anger came on like summer heat lightning; a flare in the eyes and now pure hot fury in the voice. "You should have called me and told me about Niven. I've given you some leeway here because I expect you to keep me informed."

He was cop with all cops' privileges and

powers. I told him most of the truth. "He wouldn't tell me why he's in town but it is peculiar that he got here right before Donovan got murdered."

"You've got quite a vocabulary, McCain. 'Peculiar' doesn't cover it and you know it."

Niven could still have been tailing Valerie Donovan for reasons having nothing to do with her husband's murder. I didn't believe that and Foster wouldn't either. But I wanted to keep the photograph to myself.

"He was supposed to die. Niven. The way he was worked over."

We stood aside for more folks in need of the elevator.

When we were alone again, he said, "We now have two people in the hospital."

"I thought of that myself."

"According to you, two people who are completely unrelated to Donovan's murder."

"I didn't say that. Exactly."

"He's coming around. Your friend Cullen."

"Where did you hear that?"

"Chiefs of police they keep informed. Not private investigators."

"Have you talked to him?"

"The shrink is saying possibly later this afternoon. He emphasizes 'possibly.' "

"As his lawyer, I'd like to be there if you interview him."

"Comes in handy, doesn't it? The P.I. gets to sit in on the interrogation because he's a lawyer. But I don't have to allow it."

"Are you really that pissed off at me?"

But he said nothing. Just pressed the button for the elevator.

When the doors opened he stepped aboard.

The doors closed.

Senator O'Shay, even though he might hopefully be on his way out, still had undeniable power.

He had managed to commandeer the city council, the police department, and one of our high schools to make certain that his cynical parade came off.

I had all sorts of principled reasons not to go have a look — I'm rarely happier than when I feel principled — but I walked over four blocks to the large Presbyterian church that the parade was just now passing by.

Marching band music has always embarrassed me for some reason. It's so damned *big*. But along with the embarrassment is a thrill I hate admitting to.

Heat and clamor and mothers hanging on to their little ones so they wouldn't burst into the street and dads with kids' legs wrapped around their shoulders and young couples wooing to the enormous tinny music as if it was a love song.

I looked at the faces. The faces of war. Just about everybody was in this war, either by participating directly or having a family member, near or distant, over there. You could tell the people who had soldiers over there, especially the women. Some of them cried and some of them held up their children as if to be blessed by all the people in the parade. They needed to be bound up in the swaddling clothes of what devious politicians called patriotism. Patriotism could calm your anxiety sometimes; patriotism could rock you to sleep at night; and most importantly, patriotism could quell your doubts about the worthiness of this war. My kind of patriotism — the patriotism of my generation — probably didn't count because we had as many questions as we had answers.

There weren't any floats. There hadn't been time for that. But there was a band in bright yellow uniforms, the drumline, the pomp or pomposity (your choice) of the plumed drum major. And there were convertibles, new and shiny ones on loan from the most important local dealers, and there was the mayor riding on the back of one of them followed by two uniformed soldiers on the back of another, and then a flatbed truck with a few soldiers in wheelchairs and a few more missing arms or legs. Seeing them paraded this way infuriated me and then when I saw the maroon Caddy convertible with O'Shay on the back of it I thought of what those men on the flatbed had suffered at the hands of this man and I had that fleeting Lee Harvey Oswald thought that was so much in the air these days — bang bang bang and no more O'Shay. But there were thousands and thousands more of him in our government. Ike called it the military-industrial complex but nobody had paid him much attention. And I was just a three-beer fantasy killer anyway. There were millions of us these days. With the murder of JFK, assassination was a popular game with many political daydreamers.

And then I saw him. Directly across the street.

Teddy Byrnes.

If he saw me he didn't let on. The crowd was alive as one, this great joyous animal seduced by the white-haired wizard who waved at them with papal authority.

The only satisfaction I could take was that O'Shay must have known that he was going to lose; that he would have to suffer what was for men like him a disgrace. A slender hope on my part.

And when I looked again Teddy Byrnes was gone.

I wondered if Foster was right. I wondered if Byrnes really had meant to kill Gordon Niven.

13

I sat alone in the office and called ZOOM and talked to Tim Duffy. He said he'd been discreetly asking questions of the gang that Teddy Byrnes was part of but they didn't seem to have any news about him.

I called Lindsey Shepard and lucked out. I got an answering machine for the psych clinic but when I started to leave a message she picked up herself.

"I was talking to Chief Foster this morning and he said that Will seems to be somewhat responsive now."

"That's what Dr. Rattigan told me, too. I talked to him late last night. I called this morning and was told that the chief hopes to talk with Will later this afternoon. I'm sure he wants me to tell him that it's all right but I have my doubts and so does my husband. In fact we were discussing it when you called."

"Can you stop him from interrogating Will?"

"No. I can tell him that I think this could be very harmful. If it's too intense it could send Will right back inside and then we wouldn't be able to reach him again. I'm going to call him — and Randall's going to be on an extension phone in case the chief thinks I'm just a nervous female — and give him our opinion and hope he takes it."

I heard another phone come on the line. "Maybe you could back us up on this. Give him a call yourself. Tell him you've talked with us and you hope he'll take us seriously. You seem to have a strong relationship with him."

"So do you and Lindsey."

Lindsey said, "But a call from you wouldn't hurt."

"I'm afraid right now he wouldn't be very happy to hear from me. We've had a disagreement about something and he's not too happy."

"Oh," Randall said, "that's too bad. Well, after we hang up here, we're going to call him ourselves."

"I'd appreciate it if you'd keep me posted."

"We certainly will," Randall said.

On impulse I next called Mary.

"The Lindstrom residence. Nicole speaking."

"Hi, Nicole. You do a great job of answering the phone."

"Mom trained me." I noticed Mary was "Mom" to her while to Kate she was "Mommy."

"Is your mom handy, honey?"

"I'll go get her for you, Sam. Are you coming over tonight?"

"I hope so. If I don't get too busy."

"On Saturday night Mom always makes tacos."

"I'll bet they're good."

"Thanks, honey." Mary was on the line now from the kitchen.

"I told Sam that if he came over tonight he could have tacos."

Laughing, Mary said, "I believe the legal term for that is bribery."

"I'm going to finish my book now. It's due at the library today. Bye, Sam."

"Bye, sweetie."

"It's official now. They *both* like you."

"And they say they'll give me tacos."

We spent several minutes talking about last night and then I asked her if I'd gotten any calls.

"Just one. Whoever you talked to at the hospital gave you a courtesy call back saying that Will's doctor would like you to call him."

I wrote the number down and read it back to her to be sure.

"So do I make extra tacos tonight for a certain visitor?"

"Muy tacos. Muy."

"I was in your Spanish class, remember? I'm trying to think — which one of us got the A and which one got the C?"

"Yeah, I felt sorry for you when we saw our report cards. And you'd studied so hard."

"Uh-huh."

That was when Kevin Maines walked in. His uniform today was short sleeves and walking shorts, necessary when you're dragging your ass through high eighties, high humidity as a U.S. mailman. He also wore the postal service's version of the pith helmet.

"I'll call you later, Mary."

Usually on Saturdays Kevin just shoves the mail underneath the door. Today he set three number-ten envelopes and a small manila envelope on my desk.

His light blue shirt was soaked darker blue under his pits. "Anything new on that Donovan thing?"

"Nothing that I know of."

"I know two people who used to work for Donovan. One said he was a great guy and one said he was a giant asshole."

"I suppose we've all got some of both in us."

"Yeah, my boss is like that. You never know who you're gonna meet when you show up in the morning. I could live without that kinda crap."

The number-ten envelopes contained two bills and a check from a client paying off his entire eight-hundred-dollar fee. Very nice.

The manila envelope contained three photographs and a short note. After I'd read the latter and studied the photographs, I got up and walked down the hall and got myself a Pepsi. Then I came back and went through the photos and note again.

May be in some trouble here. Hotel room
    trashed
and two threatening calls telling me to
    leave town.
You know the drill, McCain. If anything
    happens to me —

                                    Niven

I lined up the three small color photos on my desk. Each depicted the same couple in three different settings. One in a back yard

161

in bright afternoon, judging by the shadows where they were making out. The second was in a small river pavilion just at dusk. And the third was entering a motel room. In the one in a back yard he had his hand on her ass.

They had one of those relationships where enough was never enough. Valerie Donovan and Lon Anders.

I wondered what Chief Foster, aka "Paul," would make of these.

Sometimes the obvious conclusion was the correct conclusion. They're having an affair. Lon has always wanted the business to himself anyway. Like just about everybody else, he's seen *Double Indemnity* or one of its dozens and dozens of knockoffs. He knows how this sort of thing works. But he's smarter than the people in the James M. Cain novel or movie. He waits until he has the chance to make it look like a murder by someone else who seemed to have a motive. The argument between Will and Donovan was well known. So was the fight they had at the party.

What better time to murder Donovan?

This time I called Kenny.

"You ever hear anything about Valerie Donovan?"

"I heard she got it on with the tennis

instructor at the country club."

"Those tennis instructors sure get a lot of ass. Anything else?"

"The marriage was pretty rocky for quite a while. He couldn't have kids and he wouldn't let her adopt. He was also very possessive. He slept around himself. By the way, I'm looking into every single person involved in this. Anders doesn't publicize this but he's been married three times. He also went on a long weekend to Chicago with Teddy Byrnes two weeks ago."

"Isn't he on parole?"

"Not so's you'd notice."

"That Chicago weekend is what interests me most. I doubt Donovan knew about it. He wouldn't have liked it."

"Yeah, I'm sure Byrnes is a real loyal guy. Donovan's the one who helps him try to turn his life around and he throws in with the other guy."

"But Donovan got something out of helping him. He had to or he wouldn't have done it."

"What a cynical man you are, Sam McCain."

"Realistic. I know a lot of Steve Donovans."

"Well, I'll keep working. I tried you about twenty minutes ago but there wasn't any answer."

"I've had a busy morning. I watched the parade for a few minutes."

"Did O'Shay ascend into heaven in glowing robes?"

"Damn near."

"He's still going to lose. That poll in the newspaper last week really surprised me."

Five hundred Black River Fallsians were asked their opinion on the war. Sixty-five percent wanted to withdraw within a year. My town, like most of America, had had enough. It was the politicians who hadn't.

"I'll be in touch."

I spent ten minutes getting ready. I went in the john and washed my face and combed my hair and then I turned to my emergency closet. Spare sport coat, spare necktie, spare Old Spice. I always wore trousers that would look all right with the emergency sport coat if the need arose.

I stood next to my desk for a few minutes trying to plan what would be the most effective presentation. The problem was that I had no idea what I was walking into. The only thing I could count on was that it likely would not be civil. In fact it could get downright ugly. Everyone involved was under great stress and stress doesn't make for civil, rational conversations.

I knew I was putting it off because it was not anything I would even have considered if Will's future wasn't involved. I went through the photographs trying to put them in proper order for dramatic effect.

Probably the one in the back yard where they were making out. And he had his hand on her ass.

Yeah, that one would probably get her attention.

14

I was worried about mourners, family, and friends visiting or even staying overnight. Getting to her would be difficult. The best possibility was that Valerie Donovan would stay alone so Anders could slither in after dark. Or maybe even figure a way to get in during daylight.

The home was old-money gentry. A two-story brick with three-stall garage and enough chimneys to wear out Santa Claus and three gables to confuse him on a dark night. A full-size swimming pool in back as well as a screened-in porch that ran the width of the long house. This was a notable house because it had been built during the depth of the Depression by a banker who had wisely withdrawn all his cash from his place of work a month and a half before the crash. He was not exactly beloved and when he died at thirty-nine not even an O'Shay parade could have saved his reputation.

This was one of the rich people's homes my folks had driven by after Mass on Sundays. My mother had read all about it in the paper and gave us details of the interior that only a smart guide could.

No cars in the long, wide driveway. I parked and then walked to an imposing front door of intricately carved wood. The brass knocker was half the size of a basketball. I used the doorbell.

The home was isolated because of a ravine on the west side and a steep hill on the other. I tried the knocker now. Twice and then once more for luck.

She might not be home. She might be sleeping. She might be on the phone. She might not want visitors of any kind except for Anders.

I decided to try the back porch.

On my way around, a fat, cute, little brown-and-white puppy showed up to accompany me on my journey. I had to slow down because those tiny legs were churning too fast already. I stopped a couple of times to pet him. He smelled doggy good.

The porch was as advertised, an immense stone screened monument to good times for people who could afford it. The furnishings ran to expensive couches, chairs, and divans more appropriate to the interior. But there wasn't a great deal of it. Given the spaciousness of it and the flagstone floor it was easy to guess that intimate parties of fifteen to twenty privileged souls could be held here. There were small bars at both ends of the porch.

Valerie — at least I assumed it was Valerie — had her back to me as she stood talking to somebody on a phone that had a cord that would stretch the length of the place.

"No, of course I don't want to see you. I *never* want to see you." Then, "Well, you had that coming. Just because I'm trying to be cautious you tell me I don't want to see you. I'm supposed to be the bereaved widow, remember? And in fact I am feeling terrible about it." Listening. Then, "Well, you've been married three times and had sex with seventy percent of the women in this town so you wouldn't know what I'm talking about. When we were first married I loved Steve, loved him deeply. And I made a total commitment to him. So I miss him. Is that all right? And I hope that bastard who killed him doesn't get off with some kind of insanity defense. And it really does piss me off, Lon, that you don't understand a single fucking thing about making a commitment." Then, "This conversation isn't doing either one of us any good. Let's talk later."

She slammed the phone and then turned to set it on a mahogany table and that was when she saw me.

Hands on hips. "And just who the hell would you be?" A gray skirt that loved every inch of her lower body as the turquoise blouse loved the upper.

"My name's Sam McCain. We've met a few times socially."

"Must have been memorable. What the hell are you doing here?"

"I was hoping I could talk to you for a little while."

"Wait. You're Esme's investigator. Sam McCain; I thought that was familiar. I like Esme. She's one of the few people I can really talk to in this whole town. I'm sorry if I was abrupt. But I really don't want to talk right now."

"It's kind of important."

A queenly sigh. There was a cool grandness to her beauty that intimidated me. I waved the manila envelope at her and felt, for the first time, in control.

"You really should see these, Mrs. Donovan."

Hands on her hips again. "I think I'll call Esme and tell her that her little investigator is a pest. How would that be?"

I took her pause as permission to mount the three stone steps and join her on the back porch.

I waved the envelope at her again. "What I have here, Mrs. Donovan, is three photographs of you with Lon Anders. In one of them you're going into a motel room and in another he's kissing you and he has his hand on your ass."

She had a wonderful strong fuck-you laugh. "So Steve finally hired you to follow me around. Lon said he was too stupid to know what was going on. That's Lon's ego. He thinks everybody except him is stupid. So when did he hire you?"

"He didn't hire me, he hired an investigator from Des Moines. A very good one."

"So why isn't he here instead of you?"

"Somebody tried to kill him last night. He's in the hospital in bad shape."

"I suppose you want me to feel sorry for someone who was spying on me."

"I wouldn't want you to put yourself out."

"I suppose you're considered a wit."

"Just by my mom."

"I just may call Esme." The bluff was one thing she wasn't good at.

"Good. Then I'll feel free to show her these photos."

She slapped me across the ear. For all the delicacy of her face, neck, arms, and wrists, she had a slap that was three-quarters of the way to being a punch. "Sit down on the couch and let's get this over with."

My ear smarting, I obeyed her Majesty and took a seat on a peach-colored couch. She sat close but not too close. There was no way she was going to let *me* put my hand on her ass.

"Let's get this straight. You're not going to get very much money from me. I'll tell you that right now."

"I'm not here to blackmail you, Mrs. Donovan. I want to prove that Will Cullen didn't kill your husband."

"Well *of course* Cullen killed him. Who else would have?"

"Possibly Anders."

"You're being ridiculous."

"He wanted you and he wanted the business."

An amused noise. "You have it backwards. He wanted the business and he wanted me."

"That doesn't bother you?"

The same amused noise. "I forgot. You overheard me on the phone just now. Well, what you heard was me salving a very pretty man's ego. He's fun. He thinks because I've been sleeping with him — and he's very

171

skilled at that — that I'm one of those stupid little girls he's used to. He expects me to swoon every time he calls me. He's also deluded himself into believing that I want to marry him. I don't want to marry him any more than he wants to marry me. What's funny is that he's a romantic. He likes convincing himself that he's in love with certain women who just happen to have something he wants besides the love story nonsense."

"Do you think he understands that you don't love him?"

The smile of conquest. "Not right now. He's still in the romance phase. He still wants the business and me as a bonus."

"Well, he's got one of them, anyway."

"Not necessarily. With Steve gone I've now got fifty percent of everything."

"That doesn't mean he didn't kill Steve. With Will and Steve fighting, Anders saw the chance to lay the murder on Will."

"I don't believe that. I just keep thinking of poor Steve lying in that parking lot all night. And I mean 'poor' in case you think I didn't care for him. Loved him madly for a number of years, but that all got lost because he cheated on me so much. I begged him and I warned him but he wouldn't listen. So I started sleeping around myself. I could've kept a private investigator busy for years."

Then from on high: "You're a pesky little prick. I suppose some women find you cute."

"I'm too modest to comment."

An actual smile. "So if you're not going to blackmail me, what'll you do with the photographs?"

"I haven't decided. I might try them on Anders."

"Do you usually get this obsessed? I told you Lon had nothing to do with Steve's death."

"Then if you believe that, help me."

"How?"

"Don't tell him we talked. Let me try these photos on him."

"It's a waste of time but I suppose I could go along with it."

"One more thing — what did your husband think of Anders as a business partner?"

"That's the only interesting question you've asked me."

"How so?"

She sat back on the couch. The azure eyes were reflective. Her looks would not let go of me. "He loved Al like a little brother."

"Al Carmichael, his former business partner."

"Yes. They were like a couple of college boys together. The first years of the business were so successful they had plans to get as much as thirty percent of the market. Then one of their competitors invented a new spin on the basic product and Steve and Al lost market share instead of gaining it. The friendship suffered to the point that even Amanda — Al's wife — and I were cool to each other. And then Lon came along. I understand why so many people dislike him but he's a fantastic sales manager. He got profits up almost from the start. And he also made it clear that he wanted Al out and that he planned to be Steve's partner. I felt sorry for Al and Amanda and I didn't like Lon at all. But Steve did and Al was out. Just like that. Lon made things so uncomfortable for him there that one day he walked out and never came back."

"But eventually you took to Lon."

A subtle exquisite smile. "I told you he was a fantastic salesman."

She moved with instinctive grace and offered a slender hand. "I've never been in a conspiracy before."

"You're betraying Anders, you know."

"How many times do you think he's betrayed me? Sometimes I worry that he's going to give me one of those diseases he might get from all the stupid little girls he sleeps with. I was very careful in the days when I was sleeping around. Lon's never careful about anything. Part of his charm is his recklessness."

"He might have been reckless enough to kill your husband."

"I still don't believe you, but you've managed to plant a very tiny seed of doubt in my mind."

"And if I prove that he did it?"

She hesitated. Closed her eyes. And when she opened them she looked at me directly. "I'll do everything I can to see that he never leaves prison. I'll go on the stand and admit to having an affair with him and not worry about my reputation at all."

That was when the chubby, cute little dog barked. "That's Ivanhoe. Steve got him from the pound about six weeks ago. I prefer cats myself. But I have to admit Ivanhoe has ingratiated himself with me. A bit like you have with me, McCain. Even though I think you're way, way wrong about Lon."

On the way back to my car I played with Ivanhoe for a few minutes. He liked to ram headfirst into my leg as if he was trying to topple a statue.

The way I was trying to topple Lon Anders.

15

From Valerie's I drove out to Cherie's, the roadhouse where Donovan had been drinking the night he was killed. Saturday was the only day they served lunch here so the packed parking lot didn't surprise me.

I took a stool and surveyed the dining area that spread out below the raised bar. Customers generally dressed up some when they came here at night but this afternoon summer clothes, even beach clothes, were the standard.

I ordered a Hamm's draught and then asked if I could speak to Mr. Hobart, the manager.

"Something wrong, sir?"

"No, no, this is a very nice place. No complaints. This is a private matter."

"I'll need a name."

"Sam McCain."

He was mid-twenties with Beatles hair and a jaunty way of mixing drinks. He also had a good bartender's innate suspicion for anything untoward a customer might say.

"Just a second."

He stepped over to the phone next to the cash register, punched in three numbers, and then started talking in a quiet voice. He nodded and hung up and came back to me.

There were four booths in the west corner of the bar. He pointed to them and said, "Neil said to wait in one of the booths over there and he'll be out in a few minutes."

"Thanks." I picked up my draught.

A few minutes turned out to be sixteen or seventeen minutes according to my watch. The bar got more and more crowded. Most of the men along it were now watching the Cubs game on the elevated twenty-seven-inch screen.

I knew Neil Hobart from the downtown group that perpetually tried to have its way with the city council. The group was the new Establishment but they wouldn't have full power until the present group retired or passed on.

Very cool, very expensive fawn-colored collarless shirt, flowing white trousers with fawn-colored belt yet. Rimless glasses and thinning blond hair in a ponytail. How cool is too cool?

No handshake. He sat down across from

me and said, "You're wasting your time, McCain."

"I hear that a lot."

"Everything I know I told to that new police chief." I wanted to give him a quarter tip for not calling him "Paul."

"So I suppose you think Will Cullen is guilty?"

"I have a friend in the department. He laid it all out for me. Of course he's guilty. And if that isn't enough, I was at the luncheon for Senator O'Shay this noon. He's convinced it's an airtight case. That kind of says it all, doesn't it?"

"When Donovan was out here drinking the other night did you talk to him much?"

"Some. I felt sorry for the guy. This is a bullshit war and he's one of the people who paid for it. I tried to be as nice as I could but he was getting way too drunk. I did everything I could to get him to take a cab. I even offered to drive him home myself if he'd just wait till closing time."

"How was Will?"

"Sort of pathetic. He just kept drinking and saying that he wanted to be friends again with Donovan. But Donovan just kept pushing him away."

"Physically, you mean?"

"Yeah. Will'd get close and Donovan

would tell him to shut up and go away. And a couple of times he gave him a little push. No big deal. I finally got Will to go into the dining room and do his drinking."

"Was Lon Anders here that night?"

"I had a dinner that night so I didn't get out here until around nine. He wasn't here while I was. Why're you asking about Anders?"

"Just doing my job."

"Anders is a friend of mine."

"All I said was that I was doing my job and that is all I'm doing. How about Teddy Byrnes?"

A sneer as cool as his shirt. "Yeah. He was here for an hour before I got here. Then he left when I got my friend Heinrich to help me. He's one of our chefs and I had to pay a lot of money for him to come here from Chicago. Eight years ago he was still in Hamburg and he wasn't working as a chef. Have you ever heard of Sankt Georg?"

"No."

"You're taking your life in your hands to walk around there at night. Heinrich grew up there and pulled two years as a bouncer in a club where he claims there were at least two murders a month. I need any help with some psycho bastard like Byrnes, I just walk back and sic Heinrich on him. As soon as

Heinrich got Byrnes in a hammerlock and then jammed his thumb in Byrnes's eye, I assumed the fight was over. And then Byrnes slipped the hold and knocked Heinrich out in one punch. And he was out for almost ten minutes. I got scared he wasn't going to wake up."

"What happened to Byrnes?"

"He took a long look at how unconscious Heinrich looked and split."

"But he *was* here and I assume you'll testify to that."

"Of course I will. But that's a long haul to prove that he had anything to do with Steve's death. I admired Steve for serving the country, by the way, but he was totally full of shit about the war. You didn't do so well by it yourself, McCain, and you didn't even get over there. That was one hell of an accident."

"Yeah. It wasn't fun."

"I lucked out. Heart palpitations since I was young. They've never really bothered me that much but they were my ticket out so I have developed a fondness for them."

He was out of the booth and this time his hand was out.

As we shook, he said, "For what it's worth, I know Will from the times he's been out here. I like him and I feel sorry for him."

"But he's still guilty, huh?"

"I'm sorry, man," he said, "but he's still guilty."

The psych ward. I had called Lindsey Shepard but was told that she and her husband were probably on the ward now visiting with Will Cullen. I assumed I could persuade them to let me speak to Will.

I stepped off the elevator and was confronted by a long desk and two thick-looking doors to the left and right. Both bore signs: ONLY PEOPLE WITH PASSES ALLOWED. The air was somehow different here. Confined, claustrophobic.

A man in a blue security guard uniform laid his paperback down on the desk and said, "Is there something I can help you with?"

"I'd like to talk to Will Cullen but to do that I need to speak to Lindsey Shepard first. Are she and her husband here?"

The guard checked his clipboard list. "Yes, she's still here. Her husband left."

"Would you get her on the phone? I'm sure she'll say it's all right."

"I'll have to ask you for your driver's license."

"Of course." I handed my billfold over.

He studied the photo and then studied

me and then handed the billfold back.

"That's Lindsey Shepard you'd like to see?"

"Yes."

"Nice lady."

"Yes, she is."

He shook his hand as if it had been asleep and punched numbers on his phone. Then, "Kay, would you tell Mrs. Shepard that there's a man named Sam McCain who'd like to come back and see her?" Listening. "Sure, I'll hang on." Cupping the phone and to me, "Still as hot out there?"

"Feels worse than ever."

"I don't want to leave work. The air conditioning. All we've got at home are three fans. I could probably pull an extra shift if I wanted to but I'd feel guilty. I sorta feel guilty already. Here I'm sittin' in air conditioning and the wife and my three kids are sweatin' it out at home."

I heard a voice through his muffling hand.

"Yeah. Fine. I'll buzz him in right now. Thanks, Kay." After hanging up, he said, "There's a small reception area. That's what you'll be standing in when you go in there. Just wait and a nurse will come to meet you. She'll bring Mrs. Shepard to you."

Why couldn't the nurse just take me back to Will's room? What the hell was going on?

The buzz that let me in was quick and quiet. The waiting area was plastic flowers, uncomfortable-looking chairs, two tables piled with magazines, and the kind of framed paintings you can buy on the highway sometimes from trucks and people who look like stereotypical Gypsies.

I stood and waited.

Most hospital floors are busy and noisy during the day. Two corridors stretched in front of me and in the center of them was the nurses' station. I could hear conversations working their way down the halls but they were subdued; the only familiar sound was the occasional squeak of a nurse's shoe on a polished floor.

This afternoon Lindsey Shepard had shed her casual look for a summer suit of ivory-colored linen. Her hair was combed back somewhat dramatically. This more conventional Lindsey lost the appeal of her former self.

"I've tried calling you several times, Sam."

"Out and about. I just decided to run up here in case Will had started talking."

"I wish he was. I think Dr. Rattigan got a little overexcited when Will started showing signs that he was at least understanding what people were saying to him. Doctor Rattigan asked me to come over right away.

I was getting my photograph taken for a brochure we're doing. He saved me from that but I've been sitting with Will for two hours now and not getting anywhere. Chief Foster has been here twice and he's called twice. But there's nothing to report." Then, "Would you be willing to spend a little time with him?"

"Of course."

"He's sitting in a chair next to the window. The nurse said that when she first came in around seven o'clock this morning he'd gotten up out of bed and moved a chair around so he could look out. We've cut back on two of his meds to see if that might make him less groggy."

"I'll just sit there and try to talk to him."

"Hopefully he'll recognize you. And hopefully he'll trust you more than he does us. You two have been friends for years."

"A quarter century."

She hadn't lost that gamine smile. "Perfect."

Once I got to the center of the psych ward I saw that it wasn't as quiet as I'd thought. There was a group room with a large-screen TV, a ping pong table, smaller tables where both checkers and chess were being played, an exercise bike, and a tall bookcase stacked full with paperbacks. I noticed that there was a small square device in the wall near a snack table. When patients wanted to light a cigarette they went there, pressed the cigarette in what appeared to be a hole in the device and got their smoke going.

"It's a heating coil for smoking," Lindsey said. "This is the only place they're allowed to light up."

"Are you afraid of fire?"

"That's the first concern. Falling asleep with a cigarette going. But there are also patients we wouldn't be comfortable with having matches or a lighter."

A pair of the men playing chess waved to Lindsey. None of the others here took notice of her. Or me.

The patient rooms were small and functional. Bed, bureau, shower, TV, closet. Soft blue colored walls. The room had no particular odor, certainly not a hospital one. The only window was large relative to the size of the room and at a glance looked over the far east side of the town where housing developments and a sprawling mall were under construction. If there was solace in the view it would be in the distant piney hills where horses and short-haul trains still ran.

Will had angled the chair so that he could easily turn to see somebody come into his room. He must have heard us enter but he showed no interest in identifying who we were. He wore a handsome wine-colored robe. His hair was mussed. You could see that he — or more likely a nurse — had worked with a comb or brush to give it some shape but it hadn't worked.

"Will, guess who's here? This'll make you very happy."

She spoke to him as if he would respond with jovial interest. She took both sides of his chair and said, "Why don't we move you around so you two can have a nice talk?"

"Here," I said, "I can do it."

I got behind him and slid the chair around so that it faced the plain wooden chair against the west wall. His chair had thick cushions and wide wooden arms.

I stepped back then and got my first good look at him.

Though I knew this was impossible, he seemed to have lost some serious weight. Maybe ten pounds or more. Impossible. But he was so gaunt, his cheekbones sharper than they'd ever been and the flesh around his dark eyes so bruised from exhaustion they looked as if someone had punched him. He peered out at me from another realm, an unimaginable space that only he inhabited. Not the world we normally shared.

I thought of all the stories I'd heard from the vets. How wounds and grief alike would send soldiers into the kind of shock that sometimes nobody could bring them back from. They just died in that realm.

Or maybe I'd been wrong. Maybe in Will's realm he wasn't alone. Maybe the ghost of the little girl he'd killed was with him. Maybe this retreat from reality didn't have much if anything to do with Steve Donovan. Maybe it was the little girl who'd drawn him irretrievably back into himself.

"Say something to him, Sam."

I picked up the wooden chair and moved it closer to him. After I sat down, I said, "I've been thinking about you, Will. I just wanted to stop by and see how you were doing."

I felt silly. When I was very small I had a plastic Roy Rogers figure that I probably got for a box top and a quarter from whatever cereal sponsored him. It was probably six, seven inches tall and showed Roy all decked out in his fancy cowboy attire. He was then the most popular cowboy on radio and in comic books. My dad used to laugh about me talking to Roy before I went to sleep at night. Dad said I carried on a lot of one-way conversations.

Will wasn't any more responsive than Roy had been all those long years ago.

He scratched his nose, he blinked a few times, he sneezed, he sighed and he shifted in his chair trying to get more comfortable. What he didn't do was show any recognition of me in his vacant gaze.

"Remember when we beat Taylor school in softball, Will?"

Over the next twenty minutes I tried a number of those memory shakers. None worked. Lindsey had left soon after I'd started in on them. She popped back in every few minutes.

I had the feeling I was talking to an alien life form. One of those invaders who look exactly like us but are unable to pass because they don't react the way they should.

Poor Karen; even worse, poor Peggy Ann.

He narrowed his eyes once. He was assessing me, that was what it felt like anyway. He could talk but he chose not to. I was sure of it.

On her reappearance Lindsey said, "You've certainly done your best, Sam."

"I think he sort of acknowledged me at least. In his eyes. And a couple of times when I mentioned something we'd done together I saw his lips tug at the corners as if he might be trying to smile."

"That's very good news."

"So now what?"

"Doctor Rattigan has another drug he'd like to try."

"You think he knows what he's doing? Shouldn't you be in the lead here? You're a shrink."

"I should hire you to do my publicity. Doctor Rattigan is both a neurosurgeon and a psychiatrist. He'd be in a major hospital except he had a falling-out with his superior. He said, 'I'm the undisputed star here and I don't have to have fools trying to second-guess everything I do.'"

"Remind me to kiss his ring when I finally meet him."

She led me out of the room, closing the door almost silently behind her. "Randall's on his way now. We do shifts and then take breaks. He went home to take a nap. We have four other patients here so we keep busy. We quit around nine and then go home for a late supper. I finally broke down — I'm cheap — and hired a woman to cook all our dinners for us. They're there waiting in the fridge. I just pop them in the oven and we have some delicious food."

Then we were back in the waiting area.

"If there's any change I'll let you know,

Sam. But as you can see, Dr. Rattigan got pretty excited for nothing."

"Are you going to point that out to him?" The eyes were briefly winsome.

"Why, I thought you were going to do that for me."

"If I even knew what he looked like I just might do it, the mood I'm in."

"He's tall, dark, and handsome." Then, "Just ask him."

"I take it you're not a fan."

"No, not especially. But if you've been around many surgeons you know he's pretty much par for the course."

And with that she left me.

I rode down in the elevator, depressed about Will. That gaze; even when he got better I'd never forget it. The gaze was an open wound. I didn't know how Karen handled seeing him. She had to wonder if he'd ever be the same. Along with wondering if he'd ever be judged as innocent.

I stepped out of the air conditioning and into the long, hot day. The heat aggravated me.

On the drive out to Mary's I once again tried to puzzle through it all. If I could count on Valerie Donovan keeping her promise about not telling Anders that I had the photos — then confronting Anders was the likeliest move to make. He wouldn't be easy to intimidate but maybe knowing that he'd been under surveillance would damage his ego to the extent that he would make a mistake.

A long shot but everything available to me was a long shot now.

Then as I drove I started hearing the girls in my head. Their laughter. Crazy Kate and Serious Nicole. I'd enjoyed spending time with my sister's kids when I'd visited my mother in Chicago after leaving the military hospital. But they were in their early teens so they weren't as much spontaneous fun as Mary's girls.

And then I was pulling into her drive. And then Kate and Nicole were running out to meet me. And then Mary was standing on the porch in jeans, blouse, and apron waving at me with a big wooden spoon.

The girls grabbed my hands and Kate said, "I helped Mommy make the tacos."

"That means they'll be extra good, I bet."

Kate nodded and grinned and clutched my hand tighter.

I was so tired and so down, I just let them rescue me.

16

After the tacos, after the girls told me what they'd done during the day, after the one scoop of Rocky Road ice cream we each got, after Kate showed me the drawing of me she'd done, after Nicole showed me the drawing of me *she'd* done (I loved them both, even if Nicole's more resembled a human being though not necessarily me), after they were trotted in to take their baths, after they trotted out themselves in their nightshirts, after I read them *Charlie and the Chocolate Factory,* after they took a turn at drama protesting bedtime, after they told Mommy that it was me who should put them to bed, after they persuaded me to tell them a story (not half bad if I do say so myself), after I turned their light out, after they peppered me with more questions as I made my way to their door, after I made a pit stop and after I wandered back to the living room, I said, "I'm really happy they like me as much as they do, but I guess I don't quite understand why."

"I'm so tired by the end of the day I'm not always a lot of fun. And they love playing with you. Plus you're sweet with them. And it got so bitter by the time of our divorce. They really appreciate a man who is nice to their mom. Poor Nicole saw her father kissing the woman he was cheating with. He'd taken her along with him to pick up some things at the store. Then he apparently couldn't control himself and drove over to see the woman. He went inside her house and stayed longer than he apparently realized. Nicole had to go to the bathroom very badly. So she just followed where he'd gone. The house had a side door, a glass one, and when Nicole got up to it there was her dad and this woman really making out. She's never gotten over it. I sent her to a counselor. The counselor said she's making progress. I guess I've talked about you so much in the last year or so the kids couldn't wait to meet you. You're fun and easygoing, Sam. You know how my ex is. Control freaks don't have much fun in life. They're always worrying that there's somebody who's doing something they wouldn't approve of. Then one night he hit me very hard in the face."

"What? He hit you?"

"With his full fist. I had a big bruise on my left cheek. He knocked me to the floor and I think I was unconscious for a minute or so. I remember Nicole kissing me and kissing me and screaming for me to wake up. Kate was just sobbing. They really turned against him after that. But I feel so sorry for them; they're conflicted. As much as they think they hate him they still love him. That's what's so terrible about divorce. All the conflicts kids develop."

"Remind me to deck that bastard the next time I see him."

"That's what we need, Sam. More violence."

I laughed. "Well, he sure as hell has it coming."

"How about you shut up and we just watch TV?"

We were on the couch. She was in my arms. We were idly watching *The Glen Campbell Show*. Enjoying it at one remove as we necked and vaguely fooled around. I liked her looks, her flesh, her scents and most especially I liked her.

When the phone rang we had to untangle and she grabbed it with a thumb and two fingers from the table next to the couch.

"Hello." Then, "Yes, he's right here."

She handed me the receiver and then stood up to smooth down her Levi's and straighten her blouse. Without a bra she had become my goddess.

"Hello."

Lindsey Shepard. "Randall and Chief Foster are in with Will now. He's talking semi-coherently."

"What changed since this afternoon?"

"There's no way of knowing. I need to tell you something that you won't like. Chief Foster was very gentle with him but he did ask the questions he normally would in an interrogation. And when he talked about Donovan dying Will broke down. Sobbing. He just kept saying he didn't mean to kill Donovan. Chief Foster took that as a confession but I'm not sure it is. Will is so confused we had to remind him of his name a few times."

"He didn't kill Donovan."

"I know, Sam, I'm on *your* side. I'm trying to *help* Will but Foster's trying to put him in prison. I was against allowing Foster in here until we'd spent more time with Will but he insisted and finally Randall gave in and said all right."

"I wish Randall had held out longer."

"Foster puts on a good front. He pretends he's so easygoing and understanding, but when I watched him with Will this afternoon I saw the predator side of him. He stayed calm and he even apologized to Will a few times. But it was all part of his act. He's a master at head games. He led Will right into saying that he didn't mean to kill Donovan. You should have heard him. He started talking about the girl Will had killed in Vietnam and then he asked Will how he would feel if he knew that some people thought he'd also killed Donovan. Very clever. He kept working that until Will broke down and said what he said." Fatigue was her tone of voice now. She'd been there most of the day and what a day it had been. Getting nowhere and then Will suddenly speaking only to implicate himself in the killing.

"I'd better go now, Sam. Randall and I need to go home. Doctor Rattigan gave Will a heavy-duty sleeping pill."

"I hope someday Will'll be able to realize all you've done for him, Lindsey."

"How about you, Sam? Look what you're doing for him."

"Right now that feels like very little."

"All we can do is keep working, hoping."

We said our good-nights.

Mary, who was standing over me, watched me replace the receiver and then handed me a cold bottle of Hamm's. "So Will is talking?"

"Not making a lot of sense sometimes. And when he made a little bit of sense he implicated himself in Donovan's killing." The beer was magical elixir. I put the chilled bottle next to my forehead. I flashed on the military hospital, the headaches. If the mystical power of the icy glass against my head couldn't stave one off, what could?

"Feel like messing around?"

"I hate to say it, but I'm wasted."

She took my hand. "That's fine, Sam. You're not my gigolo."

The image was so comic my groin responded faintly. "Well, for now let's say that my last statement may be subject to revision."

"I'm tired myself so either way is good for me. I enjoy just sitting here with you."

I'd been involved three or four times in what I'd imagined were serious relationships but more and more I realized that this one was different. There was a comfort, an ease with Mary the other affairs had lacked. I'd always been afraid they would leave me, an anxiety that never quite disappeared. It wasn't that I took Mary for granted — she could always leave me, too — but that I trusted her. I'd known her as a friend, even as a buddy sometimes, and as a substitute girlfriend to carry me through the worst patches with Pamela Forrest, and finally as a lover. I was just more relaxed now.

So we ended up in bed about twenty minutes later. There are numerous types of lovemaking. That night we created a new kind, exhausted sex. Short and sweet, followed with her spooning me and deep, deep sleep.

Anders had built his glass-and-wood faux manse on a hill overlooking a long stretch of meadow on the north end of town. Like a good detective, I'd brought along my binoculars so I could see if his Porsche was there. And it was.

I was parked on the gravel road that ran past his place. I knew an investigator who claimed that the only way to get through a stakeout was to jerk off. He liked to tell the story that one night he had three sessions with himself he was so bored. My stakeout was less rewarding. I thought about Gordon Niven, how he was doing. I'd lost sight of him in all the pressure of other things.

But Niven didn't last long in my thoughts. I concentrated on Anders. The concrete driveway from his house to the road was narrow enough to play a trick on him. A trick that would rattle and piss him off enough to take me seriously. Laying the photos on him, I would at least become dangerous.

It took a while. Sunday morning is when the respectable ministers hit the radio. Their version of things is reasonable, compassionate. I rate everybody on my fantasy Snore-o-Meter. It goes from one to ten. Ten is when, in terms of radio, you not only turn it off, you spit at it. They were cruising along at about seven. I missed the weekday crew who had everything but rubbers to sell you in the name of Jesus and who wanted you to shoot your neighbors if you just happened to suspect they might be Satan disguised in a golfing outfit.

And then, thanks to my binoculars, he was walking out his door and heading to the double garage separate from the house.

Oh but wait . . . Who is that woman leaving his house now?

Why it's none other than . . . Valerie Donovan.

So much for being careful and endangering her reputation as suffering widow.

He backed the gleaming Porsche out of the garage and then she got in.

My plan could misfire if I was late or early by even five seconds. I was in place, my foot was on the gas and I was ready. It helped that I disliked him as much as I did. I had no doubt that he'd sicced Byrnes on Gordon Niven. Damn right I was ready.

He fired down the drive three times faster than was sensible and when he saw me he started leaning on his horn. The sound perfectly captured the rage he had for some rodent who was parked horizontally across his driveway, blocking him almost entirely. The next part wasn't pretty at all. The screech of his tires, the horn still blasting and even with the windows closed, Valerie's screams.

For the first time I realized that he might not be able to stop. He could smash into me at a good clip and all three of us would suffer for it.

But screeching, fishtailing, still using his horn, he came to a stop about five feet from my car.

Then he was out of his car with a pistol in his hand. His face was heart-attack red and his eyes deranged.

And then I was out of my car with my dad's forty-five in my right hand and the manila envelope in my left.

Valerie was still in the car. She was crying.

Anders and I faced off.

"You shoot me, Anders, copies of these photos get mailed by my secretary to the chief of police. He should be interested in you and Valerie having an affair."

"For what it's worth, I could kill you right now, you little pissant, and get away with it. You were trespassing."

"I'm on county property, you stupid fuck."

Valerie was out of the car. In a light blue dress, her dark hair catching the sunlight, she was more stunning than the day itself.

"Will you two dumb bastards put your guns away? Aren't we all having enough trouble already?"

"I want to kill this little piece of shit."

"Good for you, Lon. There've been plenty of times I've wanted to kill *you* but I didn't because I'm what you might call civilized. Now give me your gun."

"You don't know how to handle a gun."

"I know not to pull one on somebody." To me, "We could've cut you in half with Lon's car, you dipshit. And that's what you are, McCain. A pure and simple dipshit. I couldn't think of the right word yesterday. But seeing you standing there with a gun and that manila envelope the right word just came to me."

"The guy you had Byrnes put in the hospital. Byrnes figured out he was following you but he didn't figure out that Niven already had some photos of you. Niven sent

202

these to me because he was scared."

"Byrnes should've killed that bastard." Anders.

"You may get your wish. Niven's in bad shape."

"Wait a minute," Valerie said. She'd been standing close to Anders but now she backed away as if she'd discovered he was toxic. Which he was, of course. "You had that pig Teddy Byrnes put somebody in the hospital?"

"Oh, for shit's sake, Valerie, don't get into one of your sanctimonious moods as usual. I did what I needed to. He was following me around. And now I learn he got photos of us. He would've blackmailed us."

"He wouldn't have blackmailed either one of you. He's a decent guy." Me.

"How many times have I told you that I don't want you hanging around Teddy Byrnes? He's a psychopath. When he looks at me I get terrified."

"It's all in your head."

"Will you say that after he rapes and kills me some night when you're not around? And give me that damned gun."

He sighed like a diva, then handed it over.

"You too, dipshit. Bring it here."

She was proving my suspicion that she was a one-woman liberation movement.

I walked over and handed it to her. She went to my car and opened the door and dropped them on the front seat.

"What the hell're you doing?" Anders snapped.

"I'm riding back with him."

"What the hell're you talking about?"

"You may've had Byrnes kill a man."

"He isn't dead. He's just hurt."

"My God, listen to yourself, Lon. 'He's not dead. He's just hurt.' And that's supposed to make me feel better? Maybe you had him kill Steve, too." The idea that she might have been sleeping with the man who would go on to murder her husband — hiring it or doing it himself — broke her. She put both of her hands over her face and began weeping.

I reached out to touch her arm but Anders snarled at me.

"Don't you ever touch that woman. She's going to be my wife."

Her weeping became cackling. "Did you hear him?" she said to me, her mascara running slivers of black down her cheeks. "He thinks I'm going to marry him after all this?"

Then came my marching orders, albeit teary ones. "C'mon. I want you to hide me someplace where this pig can't ever find me."

"I don't believe this!" Anders was walking around in circles, throwing his hands up to the sky. "He parks in front of us and damn near kills us and you're going off with him? And he has my gun! He has my gun! This is insane! Insane!"

He was still yelling at the innocent sky when she seated herself regally in my very unregal car, the handguns in her lap.

"I can't believe I had an affair with him. I'm not stupid, am I?"

"No, you're hardly stupid."

"And I'm not a whore, am I?"

"No, I don't think you're a whore."

"Then what am I?"

"You're a woman who made a mistake is all."

"I slept with the man who may have murdered my husband. That's one hell of a big mistake."

"Well," I said, "I guess I'd have to agree with you there."

Three minutes later:

"Are you going to turn him in?"

"I can't prove he hired Byrnes to beat up Niven."

"I heard him admit it. And so did you."

"I don't know if it's enough."

"And he also may have killed Steve."

"That one he didn't admit to."

"I think he did it."

"I think so, too. But there's something I need to check out before I can be sure." Then, "No offense, but Steve could be a jerk. Beating up Will and all."

"I hate to say that with him gone and everything."

"But he could be a jerk."

"Yes; I guess I'd have to go along with that. But only sometimes. Sometimes he was the most loving man I ever knew. But then he started cheating on me — and it took its toll. It's almost as if he'd forgotten how to woo me and love me. He must've been thinking of his girlfriend all the time. And it broke my heart."

"But even though he was a jerk sometimes he was sort of a Boy Scout at the same time. John Wayne and all that stuff."

"I never told him how stupid I thought the war was. But he was an Eagle Scout when he was in high school. And at the top of his ROTC class in college. So this war — he was all my country right or wrong. What Cullen did infuriated him." Then, "Where are you going to hide me?"

"I have some friends I was thinking about. They'd be happy to make you comfortable and keep you safe."

"That sounds perfect."

But as we rolled closer to town . . .

"Do you mind if I ask where your friends live?"

"Over on Fourteenth Street and B Avenue."

"On the southwest side, then?"

"Yes."

"Hmm."

"Hmm" being her last word for at least two minutes. . . .

"I really hate imposing on people."

"Of course you do."

"And on that side of town the houses are pretty small."

"That's very thoughtful of you."

"Why thank you. I was thinking maybe it would be easier to take a suite at the Royale."

"Register under a false name."

"I didn't even think of that. Perfect." Then, "Could I hire you to stand guard?"

"I'm not sure what that means."

"You know, like a bodyguard."

"I don't think you need a bodyguard."

"He could always bring in Teddy Byrnes."

She was quite a female. So lost in herself she could insult you without even knowing it. But I admired her for mourning her husband. There I'd been wrong about her. And so I might be wrong about her fear of

Anders. He really had looked insane back there at the bottom of his driveway.

"I know a couple of cops who'd sit in your room and keep you safe when they're off-duty. You'd have to pay them of course."

"But they're police officers. Why would I have to pay them?"

"Off-duty, I said."

"Well how much would it be?"

"Say five bucks an hour."

"That could turn into a lot of money."

"That's what supermarkets pay them to direct traffic on weekends."

"When you have money people are always trying to take advantage of you."

"Those bastards," I said. "Those dirty bastards."

I guess my humor wasn't to her taste. She didn't laugh.

17

They wouldn't let me talk to Will, so since Gordon Niven was in the same hospital I visited him.

He looked like most of the cartoons I've seen depicting some badly injured person in the hospital. Bandaged enough to make a passing reference to Boris Karloff as "The Mummy."

"Remember now," the nurse said as she left, "he can't talk. The doctor put him in a coma."

I pulled up a chair and sat next to him. I had a brief fantasy of taking a machete and dividing Byrnes into five slices.

The room was a single and even for a single a small one. Someone had placed a black rosary on his bandaged white hand. He was so gauze-wrapped it was hard to see any breaks or bruises. He slept. He was a mummy.

"I'm going to get that bastard for doing

this to you."

I looked around the room. Painting of Jesus on the west wall. For once he wasn't pretty. Niven's travel bag sat under the elevated TV set. He mumbled something and I instantly snapped my head around. Was he waking up?

I sat very still and listened. More mumbling but I had no idea if he was trying to say something or these were just noises inspired by things going on in his mind. I sat there for maybe ten minutes, then I decided to check out his travel bag.

Socks, underwear, shaving supplies, two folded golf shirts yellow and green, two small photo albums of Niven and a woman who was presumably his wife and their kids and grandkids, a paperback edition of *The High Window* by Chandler (I smiled when I remembered the discussion we'd had about Chandler), and then — the surprise — the same kind of back-pocket notebooks I used. Four of them lay on top of a tape recorder not much larger than the paperback.

I lifted the notebooks out and started reading them.

Like most of us in the business he date-lined everything. 8/11/71. And then writing that was largely in code. Since the words were meant only for him, he didn't care if anybody else could read them. Hell, he didn't *want* anybody else to read them.

One day he had trailed Anders for nine hours. There was one sentence that made me wonder if Anders was cheating on Valerie. He'd gone into a new "Singles Only" apartment house and stayed for three hours.

That same night he followed Anders back to his business. Anders was inside about forty-five minutes and then he appeared in the parking lot with Donovan. "Anders shoved him; Donovan swung on him." But he couldn't pick up what the two men were arguing about.

Then I found a page that was a back-grounder on Anders.

Interview at local airport: Anders flies his plane frequently. Colgan Air Services.

Keeps a woman in Cedar Rapids condo.

In default on child support wives one and two.

Has resisted all attempts to buy into his operation or to buy him out.

"I hope you find those notebooks more useful than I did. He's never let me look through them."

I turned to find a woman of about sixty

who was svelte and knowing but with charitable blue eyes and a hint of a smile. The gray chignon, the elegant cut of the gray dress were a perfect match for the slight air of superiority that celebrated the fact that she was still a stunner at her age.

I set the notebooks down. "I apologize. I'm nosy by profession. I'm a private investigator, too. My name's Sam McCain."

"I should have introduced myself." She stepped smartly to me and took my hand. "I'm Gordon's wife. Are you a friend of his?"

"I just met him. But I've been hearing about him for years."

"Well, take some advice from me. Don't ever try to figure him out. I've been married to him for thirty-three years and I never could find out what he's all about. Our children say the same thing. You can never tell what he's going to do next. I don't think *he* even knows what he's going to do next." Another glance at him. The voice wan now. "There's a good chance he won't make it." Then, "I drove down as soon as the hospital called me. I could barely concentrate on my driving. I didn't want him to die before I could at least kiss him one more time." Then, "He should've quit six or seven years ago. I begged him." Then, "Do you know who did this to him?"

"I think I do."

"Can you prove it?"

"No, not yet."

"Is that person still in town?"

"Yes. He's a psychopath. But I just promised Gordon that I was going to get the man who did this to him. One way or another."

"You sound sure of yourself."

"I am."

"Aren't you afraid?"

"Do I look afraid?"

"Well," she said, "since you brought up the subject, you actually do."

I laughed. "You're a very perceptive woman."

Colgan Air Services was set right on the edge of the city limits. It was standard for the kind of business you usually saw attached to larger airports. Here you could rent aircraft, take flight instruction, fuel up, use a hangar, tie down your craft, or even take a nap in a small room Billy Colgan made available.

Billy was a short and short-fused Irisher who had enough hair on his arms to make an ape envious. I'd never seen him in long-sleeved shirts. Maybe all that hair needed to be aired out.

You walked past a row of tied-down small craft to reach a round yellow metal building that housed the office as well as one of two hangars. Billy's wife Mara was one of the fastest typists I've ever seen. She was plain until she smiled. Then she was striking. She paused in her assault on her typewriter keys to see me and smile. Like Billy and all his employees she wore a tan short-sleeved shirt with Colgan Air above the breast pocket.

"Hi, Sam. Billy'll be glad to see you. He wants his chance to win back that forty dollars he lost last time you and Thibodeau and Father Brogan played poker. But I guess Brogan won even more than you did."

"He cheated."

She had a cheerful, bawdy laugh. "Right, Sam. A priest who cheats at poker."

"He does."

I'd been trying to convince our revolving group of players that Father Brogan was a cheater since he'd joined us a year ago. They refused to believe it but it was true.

"That's the kind of talk that'll send you to hell for sure."

"I've already booked passage."

She was still smiling. "A priest who cheats at poker," she said as she raised Billy on the intercom.

Billy came around his desk as if he was

going to grab me and throw me to the ground. He was best known to the boys of Catholic school as the all-time arm-wrestling champion. This had started in third grade when he'd beaten a fifth-grader. You didn't want to be around him when he was drunk because the fun would stop at some point while he insisted that every male in the room arm-wrestle him. Arm-wrestling is interesting for about one minute and four seconds.

"Great t'see ya, Sam. Siddown."

The flying he'd picked up in high school. It had been called Parker Air then. Billy had convinced old man Parker to let him work here and in between moving planes around, scrubbing toilets, and watching Parker give flying lessons — sometimes to comely young women — he got the fever. No college for him. He got his pilot's license and started flying cargo out of St. Paul and then when old man Parker decided to retire, Billy managed to get enough of a bank loan to make a serious down payment on the place. Old man Parker had let him pay off the rest from profits.

After we were seated, Billy said, "Poor Will, huh?"

"He didn't do it."

Genuine surprise played on his broad

215

face. "You might be the only one who thinks so."

"There're some others."

"I'm getting the sense that this isn't a social visit."

"Afraid it isn't, Billy. I want to know a few things about Lon Anders."

"You think *Anders* had something to do with this?"

"I can't say yes and I can't say no at this point. That's why I need to ask you some questions."

"Before you start, Sam, Anders is a good customer."

"I just want to ask a couple of simple questions."

He shrugged. "As long as I don't think I'm violating a confidence."

"Fair enough. How often does he fly?"

"About average for my business. Two, three times a month."

"Business or pleasure?"

"Half and half or so. He loves taking his ladies up and scaring the shit out of them. Getting into dives and pretending he's stalled. Things like that."

"He ever get in trouble showing off like that?"

"No. But I've warned him plenty of times. He's a good pilot but not a great one. One

216

of these days he's going to be clowning around like that and not be able to get control back."

"Ever see him take up Valerie Donovan?"

"Bad question."

"Cathy Vance?"

"Another bad question."

"How about where he goes?"

"He's got a thing about Denver. Shacks up there a lot."

"Ever leave the country?"

"You sure ask a lot of bad questions."

"So he does leave the country."

"You said that, I didn't. And you're only guessing."

"I'm trying to save Will here, Billy."

Now he waited me out. "Will's our friend, Billy."

"Not mine."

"What the hell are you talking about?"

"He's never been especially friendly to me, Sam. And I'm talking way, way back. I think it was because of my old man."

Billy's old man, along with two other of his Navy buddies from the big war, had stuck up a bank. Even in the Hills that had marked the family as outsiders.

"He ever say anything directly?"

"He didn't have to, Sam. I'm not exactly an idiot, man. I can tell."

"So you won't help him even though he's innocent."

"You have to be careful about people saying they're innocent, Sam. Just before he started doing time my old man told me *he* was innocent, too. No offense, but I gotta get back to work here."

I joked a little with Mara on my way out. I should've gone straight to the parking area but I veered right and went to the stand-alone hangar.

Marv Serbosek was working on a newer model vintage Piper Cub. He stood on a three-step ladder. An ear-numbing version of *Proud Mary* with Ike and Tina Turner was keeping him entertained. The noise bounced off the metal walls.

I had to yell twice to catch his attention.

Marv had been in a beard-growing contest at the county fair last summer. He had yet to unburden himself of the gray-flecked reddish thing that reached the upper pockets of his overalls.

"Hey, McCain. How's it goin'?"

"I was wondering if you could help me with something."

"Sure. If I can." His mother and my mother had been longtime members of the local Catholic church. It was the only connection Marv and I had but I hoped it was enough.

"You know Lon Anders, right?"

"Mr. Anders? Sure. What about him?"

"He ever fly out of the country?"

"Oh, yeah. Two, three times a year he goes to Mexico. Guess a friend of his has a house down there. Why?"

"Well, I was talking to Billy and he didn't want to give me any information about Anders."

The long, narrow face grew taut and the brown eyes showed fear. "Hell, I might be in trouble now. You shoulda told me that, Sam."

"I won't say anything to Billy if you don't. I wasn't trying to get you into any trouble, Marv. And I'm sure you won't be in any trouble if we keep this between ourselves."

He managed to mumble agreement but I could see that now we didn't have any connection at all. He felt betrayed and even if I was pretty sure Billy would never find out I didn't blame Marv at all for feeling used.

18

That afternoon we took the girls to a movie.

There was only one we were under sacred obligation to see and that was *Willie Wonka & the Chocolate Factory.* On the way to the theater Kate was so rhapsodic about seeing it that Nicole finally started singing to shut her up.

Twenty minutes into the movie Kate climbed up on my lap and went to sleep.

The movie was only one of the subjects we discussed when we used the outdoor grill in the back yard to make burgers. I even made a couple burgers myself and nobody died.

In the long twilight everything slowed down and quieted down and for once the melancholy I usually felt at dusk eluded me. It was touching to hear the girls slowly slip into exhaustion. To hear Kate this subdued was a revelation. She asked her sister to tell her the rest of the movie when they went to bed that night. Mary was quiet as usual. She always joked that who needed TV when you had the two girls. She loved watching them together. So did I.

I had to carry Kate inside. She was out. Mary revived her for the bath and the good-nights and the prayers and then the lights-out.

"I am so lucky to have them," she said when she came back and sat next to me.

"You sure are."

I got a bottle of Hamm's from the fridge and went into the living room and we watched a rerun of an old Jackie Gleason series, *The Honeymooners.* Gleason was always good but the woman who played his loving and lovely wife and the guy who played his bumbling buddy were just as good. The desperation of their lives reminded me of growing up in the Hills. All those men back from the big war trying to work their way out of poverty while their wives cut every corner they could while trying to raise their kids right. The show was sad fun but fun nonetheless.

I grabbed the phone when it rang.

"I'm trying to reach Sam McCain."

"That's me. Help you with something?"

"My name's Cliff Donlon. Tim Duffy's a friend of mine from bowling league. I was talking to him and he gave me this number and said I should call you. I worked for Steve Donovan. I did not work for Anders."

"That's an interesting distinction since they were full partners."

"I was with Steve from the beginning. He changed a lot when Anders came along. I almost quit when Al Carmichael left. Al was a great guy. Anders ran him out and Steve let it happen. But I stayed. Since Steve is gone I want to talk to somebody about something that's been going on there ever since Anders came."

"And what would that be?"

"I'd rather meet for an early breakfast. I need to be at work by eight so how about meeting me at McDonald's at seven? The one on the east side."

"I'll be there, Mr. Donlon. And thank you very much for calling."

19

McDonald's was still something of a novelty for our town.

A local land baron had a young daughter who'd made him drive her to Iowa City every week to pick up a huge sack of burgers and fries which would be stored in the family fridge and then heated up whenever the teenager desired. The local land baron decided it would not only save him from driving into Iowa City for the stuff, it would be downright profitable if he owned the franchise himself. Instant McDonald's.

Donlon waved me over, a redhead of forty or so in a gray worker's uniform, a long, wiry body and a pair of savvy blue eyes that were street-smart and withholding of judgment on everything that passed before them. He had a quick, iron handshake.

I set my thousand calories down across from his and sat down. We had to speak up to be heard above the packed house.

"The wife says this stuff puts the weight on me. But you can't prove it by my scale. I weigh about what I did when I was in high school. She also says it's a lot cheaper to eat breakfast at home. But I'm addicted to this stuff."

"It's pretty good."

"I'm kinda in a hurry to get to work so I'll get right to it." Quick sip of coffee. "I was one of Steve's first employees. His dad had been in the Navy and so had I. Steve liked that and so we got along very well. Till Anders came into the picture. He got rid of Al first of all and Al had been just as nice to all of us as Steve had been. Steve gradually got to be pretty much like Anders. And Anders was making most of the decisions. You could tell that, everybody could. Steve'd start to say something and Anders'd just interrupt him. Sometimes Steve would just take it but sometimes they'd argue right in front of everybody. Or they'd go into one of their offices and then they'd *really* argue. I missed the old Steve and so did everybody else who worked there. Then Anders made me start making these runs for him."

"What kind of runs?"

"To this cabin he had that nobody was supposed to know about. He said he'd fire me if I ever told anybody about what I was doing."

"Doing?"

"Yeah, loading up maybe twenty of our shipping boxes — the medium-sized ones — and then running them out to the cabin. I also took along packing material for shipping. I thought it was strange. We have our own shipping department and those women are damned good at what they do. So I was always kinda curious about it. Then Steve gets killed."

"You're making some kind of connection?"

"I'm just saying the way those two have been going at it lately — well, Tim Duffy told me that this Will Cullen is a friend of yours and you don't think he did it, so I thought I'd let you know about these runs I make for Anders."

"How often would you say?"

Between the milling people waiting in line, the tables and booths swollen with people and the speaker announcing orders that were ready every few minutes, the noise had risen even higher. A relaxing, cordial atmosphere setting just the right ambience for dining on the exquisite cuisine. I'd always prefer the mom-and-pop diners I'd grown up with.

"Three, four times a year."

"Tell me about the cabin."

"Pretty fancy." He then went into detail.

"Where's it located?"

He slid a clear pencil-drawn map on a sheet of plain white paper across the table to me.

"You did a hell of a good job with this."

"Thanks."

"When's the last time you went out there?"

"Two weeks ago. And when I did, Steve was waiting for me when I got back. He told me I was never to do this again. And that was when Anders shows up and the two get into this shouting match. It was right near the loading docks in the middle of the day."

"What happened after that?"

"I just went back to work. I saw Steve get in his car and drive off. He peeled out pretty fast. I felt sorry for him. A lot of people didn't like him but I did. He was a hard worker and a good boss. Anders is a lazy sonofabitch. I already put my application into two factories yesterday. I won't work for him under any conditions. Steve and Al built that business, he didn't."

"You have any idea what your trips were about?"

"Not really. But I don't figure it was

anything legal."

"Doesn't sound like it."

"I guess we pretty much agree that Anders had something to do with Steve's death."

"Now I have to prove it."

"Anything I can do, just let me know." He checked his watch. "Guess I'd better hurry up and eat. I hate to go back there with Steve dead and all but I need to make sure I get all the money that's due me so I'd better be on time."

He finished his food and then did away with his coffee. "Wish I didn't like this stuff so much." His one and only smile.

"Like I said," he said as he grabbed his gray lunch pail, "anything I can do, you keep me in mind."

The Wentworth apartments were the first in town to offer a swimming pool, a game and dance room, and owner-sponsored parties in said game and dance room once a month. They'd been built three years earlier, four three-story buildings of stucco and wood treated to look like driftwood. A singles place but, unlike its competition for the singles crowd, they didn't make a point of it in their advertising.

As I walked to the manager's office — Tom Wentworth had small real estate offices all over town; Cathy Vance's was right here where she lived — I passed along the pool where eight young women (I counted them) lay in lounge chairs. They wore bikinis of various colors and hairstyles of even more variety. A speaker hidden somewhere above the office played *Me and Bobby McGee.* Janis sounded as wasted as I felt. I had no doubt that Will was innocent, I had no doubt that he was worth every second I put toward proving him innocent, I had no doubt that we'd be good friends for the rest of our lives.

But I sensed his relationship with Cathy Vance had been much more serious than either of them had let on. Right now all I knew was that he'd badly damaged his wife. His daughter would be next. She wouldn't understand it now but three or four years down the line she'd begin to know what had, in all likelihood, driven her parents apart. The stats on divorces on returning vets were so bad that Congress had done what they always did, ordered a committee to study it.

I could see Cathy through the front window marked Wentworth Real Estate. In a tight black skirt and red blouse, her Ava Gardner hair flung back with contrived abandon, she perched on the corner of her desk, a receiver between ear and shoulder, the long fingers holding a cigarette that coiled blue smoke into the office air.

She watched me walk into her office with those wary silver-blue eyes of hers. The terrible thing that had happened to her that night in the Hills would always deny her the cachet of a true femme fatale. She'd been raped by two older men who'd been drunkenly stumbling home. That they served long prison terms didn't matter much to a girl of twelve. Her cynicism was the product of pain, not arrogance. She broke too easily.

"You asked for my opinion, Nick, and I gave it to you. I think they're asking way too much for that land. I'm halfway convinced he's even making up those rumors about a big office building being planned for there." There was no smile for me but she did point to the small buff-colored leather couch in the far corner. "Nick, we're friends. I'm not saying you don't know what you're doing.

"We all misjudge things. I'm right about three out of four times at best. So you shouldn't take what I say personally. All right?" Then, "Nick, a customer just came in. Just think about what I said. I could always be wrong about this and you could always be right, all right?"

229

She hung up. "I don't care what they say. You boys are way more vain than us girls. The guy calls me for an opinion and I give him an honest answer and he's hurt. I offended his manliness somehow." The showgirl smile. "But then I guess I can't blame him. He doesn't have much manliness to spare."

Four desks, walls covered with photos of homes and businesses and properties for sale. The furnishings and the carpeting ran to variations on brown.

"I imagine you're here to pester me about Will some more. And by the way, I see you've done a fine job of proving how innocent he is."

"I'm doing the best I can."

"I'm sure that's a great comfort to him."

"Did he ever write you any letters?"

"Yes, he did as a matter of fact. Before she stole him from me that summer in college. I used to think that maybe he was going to be a writer."

"More recently, I mean. When you were having an affair with him."

"You're still on that."

"His wife found some letters he wrote to you but apparently never mailed. Recent letters."

"I imagine she had a fine time reading

them. The same fine time I had reading his letter that he was breaking off our engagement."

"That was a long time ago."

"Maybe for you. Not for me. I still remember basically going to bed for a month and not being able to get up. I started thinking that the shock had paralyzed me. I was that nuts. I got over that part of it but there was a part that stayed with me. And it's with me now. Two husbands and two shrinks later and it's still with me."

"So you had an affair with him."

She was leaning against the desk facing me. In her languid, enigmatic way her sexual powers were undeniable. But the silver-blue eyes never quite gave you any hint of what she might be thinking. There was even a possibility that she did not understand her own erotic force.

"Yeah, Sam, we had an affair. And yes, he wrote me some letters. It's nice to know that he wrote some that he didn't even mail. Which makes me wonder why he broke it off."

"Well, it could always be that he was married."

"I know you think that's a smart remark but that's not why he broke it off. He didn't love Karen anymore. He made that plain. I

231

wanted him to leave her and marry me. For me the affair was like being in college again. I even let some of my work go, which I never do. But I didn't care. We got together every chance we had. We even used to meet at seven thirty in the morning sometimes. He always joked how good morning sex was in a sleazy motel. Then it ended. And he broke it off the same way he'd broken it off the first time. No explanation. Just 'I can't do this anymore.' No warning whatsoever. I'd had to find out about Karen by myself. And it's the same this time. No idea."

She walked around behind her desk and sat down. She helped herself to a cigarette. "So you got what you wanted, Sam. I admitted that we had an affair."

"When did he tell you that it was off?"

"Lunch. 5/29/71. 12:30-1:39 p.m. I put it on my calendar when I got back just the way I would any other business meeting. Because that's how he was. All business. We could have been closing on a house the way he was. He has a cold side, you know."

"Yeah, every once in a while it comes out. You rarely see it. That's what makes it so strange when you do see it. You can't equate it with this big, lumbering, smiling guy."

"But it's there. I've seen it twice now. The first time was when I started following him

232

places when I learned about Karen that summer. He wasn't just cold. He was so hostile. It was like we'd never been in love. I was just a nuisance to him."

"I'm sorry, Cathy."

The Vegas smile. "You are? The last time you saw me I didn't pick up on any great sympathy."

"Then I apologize."

She knew how to exhale cigarette smoke dramatically. "I hear you're seeing Mary Lindstrom."

"Right."

"I always envied her. She's so beautiful but it never went to her head. In fact in high school the popular girls thought she was such a loser. And I know she didn't date much because she had this thing for you. And you had it for Pamela. God, talk about a girl who was stuck on herself. You're lucky to be with Mary now."

"I realize that more every day."

Then she said it and I wasn't prepared for it and maybe she wasn't either.

"Since I'm going to confession here I may as well lay it all out for you. You were right: I sent Will those threatening letters."

"Wow."

"I told you I went a little crazy."

"That's more than a little crazy."

"He deserved it for what he did to me."

"I have to ask you, Cathy, what were you doing the night Steve Donovan was murdered?"

"God, I'm sick of talking to you, Sam. I really don't like you anymore."

"I'm sorry for that, Cathy. I really am. But I need to know where you were the night Donovan was killed."

"I didn't have anything to do with Donovan's murder. Period."

"You're not making my work any easier. I'll have to tell Foster that you sent those letters."

"Paul?" Amused. "Paul's taken me to dinner twice. Very nice guy. His wife dumped him for a younger man last year. He knows a little about the subject so he's easy to talk to."

"We've all been dumped, Cathy. And most of us survive and get past it."

"I never understood why you held on to Pamela so long. She led you around like a little dog. All those years you wasted on her. She was never going to fall in love with you and everybody could see that except you."

"You're changing the subject."

"No, I'm not. I'm just tired of you trying to make me sound like I'm the only one who held on too long. You don't think that there are a lot of married people who are still in love with somebody from their past who broke their hearts?"

I eased up from the couch. "It bothers me that you sent Will those letters."

"There isn't anything I can do about that."

"The county attorney could file charges against you."

"You're going to tell him, of course."

"I have to. I should also tell Foster. But since you're such good friends, I'll let you do the honors."

"I don't care," she said, torment faint but real in her tone. "I should leave this town anyway. Every place I look I see bad memories. It's no place for me anymore."

She might have murdered Donovan, I thought. Those long-ago men and my confusing friend Will had stolen all her kindness and tenderness and compassion. She just might have framed Will. Bitterness and rage were the only things they'd left her with.

The only things.

20

The whisper war started while I was setting the table for supper.

Kate and Nicole sat hypnotized by the TV in the other room and I was tending to plates, glasses, cups, silverware, and napkins when Mary came in with a spoonful of pasta sauce for me to taste.

"Delicious."

She poked me. "You'd say that even if it was terrible, wouldn't you?"

I poked her back. "Probably."

I slung my arm over her shoulder and strolled back into the kitchen with her.

"I met that man this morning."

"Donlon? The one you told me about last night?"

"Um-hm. Nice guy and very helpful."

"Anything the police should know about?"

"Not quite yet. I want to do something before I call Chief Foster."

In the kitchen window long pre-dusk

shadows. The first stars; a large passenger plane soaring toward the half-moon; a TV tower in the distance blinking red signals into the half-night. Mixed with this were the aromas of the kitchen — the scents of pasta, sauce, coffee, and the fresh bread Mary loved to bake.

She was in the process of using a fork to test the progress of the pasta boiling in the metal stockpot on the gas stove. "What is it you want to do?"

"Donlon says that over the years Lon Anders has had him deliver shipping materials to this cabin he owns. Donlon thinks there's something illegal going on. So do I. I thought I'd check it out tonight."

She went back to pulling strands of pasta from the boiling stockpot and then nibbling on them. "Sounds like something Foster should be doing. Since he's the law and everything."

"I probably won't have much trouble getting inside."

She set down the fork she'd been using to waggle pasta strands from the stockpot and faced me. Workday weariness and apprehension and an anger she was trying not to give in to — all of these played across her face. "Have you given any thought to what you'll do for a living?"

"What're you talking about?"

"When Foster finds out he'll undoubtedly ask for your license to be lifted. And what will the state board think about a lawyer breaking and entering? You always liked that job you had in high school, bagging groceries. Maybe you could get that back."

"I'm hungry!" Kate announced as she raced into the kitchen.

"Honey, go get your sister and you both sit down and by then I'll be bringing out supper."

"Nicole said you brought home ice cream. She saw it."

Mary swept her up. "Your sister is a very good spy. But it's not ice cream. It's sherbet."

"What's sherbet?"

"You'll just have to find out. But you'll love it. Now go get your sister."

She set Kate down. Kate said to me, "Do *you* like sherbet, Sam?"

I patted my stomach. "I love it."

And then she was running away in that awkward, endearing way of hers, shouting, "Nicole, we're having sherbet tonight!"

This was when the whispering started. The girls would be near us now.

"I thought you cared about us."

"You know damned well I do. Don't pull

238

this on me."

"All right. Then I'll just say Please don't do this, Sam. You know what kind of guy Anders is. Think of us."

Nicole said, "Is everything all right, Mom?"

She'd caught us gritting whispers back and forth.

"Everything's fine, honey. Please go get your plate and tell Kate to get hers, too. I'll dish you up some pasta."

"I'm not sure I like sherbet."

"Oh, you'll like this."

"Eve had it one night for dinner. I didn't like the taste."

Easy for Mary to take a cheap shot here, but she declined. Bad woman Eve, the one who stole your dad from me, of course her sherbet would taste bad. "There're a lot of different flavors of sherbet, sweetie. This one is peach. Remember how much you like peaches?"

That satisfied Nicole and off she went to supper.

For the next half hour not even the whisper war was allowed. Only angry looks from Mary and me trying to appear misunderstood and innocent.

The girls were put to bed early — under much protest from Kate who insisted it was "still light out" — with Mary staying with them at least twenty minutes.

A beer would've tasted good; I hadn't had any alcohol all day. But I knew about the cabin now and I needed to be sober when I got inside.

When Mary came back I said, "I need to do this for Will."

"Then at least call Foster."

"I don't have the faith in Foster you do. He's like too many cops I've known."

Significantly, she sat in the armchair across from me. "Everybody I know likes him."

"Oh, he's likable and all that. But he's still the kind of cop who gets fixated on one suspect and won't consider anyone else."

"I know how much you care about Will, Sam. And so do I. But you have to agree that things look bad for him."

"I know how bad they look, Mary. But that still doesn't mean he's guilty."

"Oh, God, Sam."

She came over and drew her legs up on the couch and put her head on my shoulder.

"Not fair." Her warmth, her flesh, the scent of her hair. I wanted to forget the cabin.

"Of course it's not fair. Look what I'm up against. An obsessed man who's too stubborn to ask the police for help."

Then she really got not fair. She sat up and took my face in her hands and gave me the kind of savage kiss that was more redolent of desperation and fear than sex.

I had to push away and stand up.

"Then you're really going?"

"I'm really going."

I went into the bathroom and closed the door. Usually about this time I went upstairs and peeked in on the girls from the doorway. Their soft snoring and their Big Bird nightlight and the dolls and stuffed animals they both slept with. My attachment to the three of them grew tighter every day. The girls would be as terrified as their mother if they could understand what I was going to do. As Mary had pointed out, the real danger was in the legal ramifications of what I proposed to do. I could indeed find myself out of a job. An unemployed step-dad was a real drag.

But searching the cabin was the logical end result of my entire investigation. There was no guarantee that I would find anything incriminating there but I still needed to do it.

I stopped in the kitchen and drew a quick but precise map to the cabin for Mary. When I got back to the living room I handed it to her. She glanced at it.

"I wish you were Batman. Then I wouldn't be worried so much."

"I wish I was Batman, too. This would be easy for him."

She'd been waiting right outside the bathroom door the way Kate did sometimes when she just couldn't get enough of me.

"Do I get a kiss, Sam?"

"Let's see now — a kiss —"

If we'd gotten any more passionate we would have ended up on the floor. But once again I eased out of the embrace.

"I'm going to say some prayers."

"It couldn't hurt." And then right there as I moved toward the side door I felt a ridiculous sadness. I even had a moment when I resented Will a bit. My life would be so easy if I didn't have to worry that he'd be sent to a mental hospital and then to prison.

For life.

■ ■ ■ ■

PART THREE

■ ■ ■ ■

"It's wave after wave of planes. You see, they can't see the B-52 and they dropped a million pounds of bombs . . . I bet you we will have had more planes over there in one day than Johnson had in a month . . . each plane can carry about ten times the load a World War II plane could carry."

— Henry Kissinger

21

The night, as I knew it, vanished.

The houses, the stoplights, the store lights were gone as soon as I found the turnoff Donlon's map led me to. The road was gravel and tall summer corn walled me in on both sides. The quarter-moon hung low and stark. The day had cooled sufficiently so I kept my window down. I also kept the radio off. On the passenger seat were a cop-sized flashlight and my dad's forty-five.

I thought about Karen. The affair Will had had with Cathy Vance had made me think even more of her and less of Will. She was apparently able to justify it to herself because of his terrible experience in Nam. I tried to do that, too, but somehow I couldn't. Then I smiled to myself. Monsignor Sam McCain was doing it again, judging people from on high. I was in no position to judge Will. Not after what he'd been through.

A sudden wind tasted and smelled of impending rain.

The intersection of rural gravel roads I was looking for was several yards from a narrow wooden bridge that spanned a ravine. I found it and turned right.

More walls of corn, more gravel banging off my car.

Ahead I saw the silhouetted line of trees that marked the long area of woods I wanted. Hidden somewhere in there was Anders's cabin. I sped up.

A few times I glanced at the forty-five. Would I actually shoot and maybe kill somebody?

One more turn and I was facing the narrow lane almost lost in the barrier of looming pine trees. I cut my headlights.

To reach the cabin you traveled a dirt path that was potholed as if by intention. I had to slow to under ten miles an hour to keep from being bounced to the ceiling and cracking my head. My window was rolled up again. Mosquitoes dive-bombed in squadrons.

Donlon's map indicated that this dirt lane was approximately a quarter mile from the cabin. I kept close watch on my odometer. When I'd covered about half that distance I swung off the road and parked in an open area just wide enough to accommodate my car. I grabbed the gun and the flashlight, then got out. I locked my car and set off.

The woods provided a cacophony of sounds, some sweet, some vulnerable, some threatening. Animals of various kinds prowling, feasting, hiding.

Even among the cathedral-like trees the scent of rain was still sharp. The other sharp smell came from the pine trees.

Just before I reached the cabin I came to an open area in the woods. The grass had been mown for one thing and for another there was a green, white-trimmed wooden gazebo sitting arrogant and citylike in the middle of this nowhere.

The "cabin" lay to the right of the gazebo and it was not a cabin at all. It was a summer home, of course, two stories of wood and stone with a long, screened-in porch covering the front. The people who owned expensive places like these liked to take pleasure in dubbing them "cabins." Rustic, you know.

As soon as I reached the clearing some cosmic force threw the switch on my paranoia. I felt observed. I started studying the darkened windows under the dormered roof. They reminded me of the paperback gothic novels my sister was always reading.

Ominous, rife with suggestions and secrets. Her husband joked fondly that she bought them four and five at a time.

The quarter-moon provided enough light that I didn't need my flashlight even as I got within a few feet of the house. I stood and listened for any sound I could hear above the familiar sounds of the wooded night.

I walked to the side of the house. I'd wondered how you got vehicles in and out of here. The din of a highway explained it.

Behind the house another wide dirt path began. It ran across a stretch of meadow leading to and over a hill on the other side of which was the access road. Two ways in and out.

There were no cars around.

I went back to the screened-in porch. I still had that feeling of being observed but by now I knew it was the situation that rattled me. After all, I was committing a crime.

My clients have paid me in a variety of ways. In lieu of actual currency I've been gifted with clothes, food, tune-ups, a banjo, photography lessons, and of course Jamie. Another of my gifts was a three-piece set of burglary tools. Occasionally I'd taken them out and practiced with them on locks at my apartment and at the office.

This was my first time for real. I tried not to think about it being a Class Six Felony.

I had no trouble getting inside.

The first few minutes I spent scanning the place with my flashlight beam. Anders lived well. A huge fieldstone fireplace with what appeared to be hand-tooled pokers (but of course); expensive hardwood flooring; an outsize TV screen mounted on the west wall; this a prosperous man's idea of roughing it — the kind of pad that would give Hugh Hefner wet dreams. A little Frank on the stereo and the woman would be tearing her clothes off before she'd put even one three-inch high heel on the outside steps.

I had passed a partially open closet door and had started toward a hallway that I assumed would lead to the kitchen. I heard the closet door behind me make a faint but unmistakable sound. I spun around. He charged at me tiger fast and tiger sure. I was prey, long-awaited prey.

I raised the forty-five to fire but before I could he'd slammed into me. The gun hadn't even slowed him down. He was so sure of himself he knew slamming into me would knock it from my hand. As it had.

His massive hands did not intend to just choke me to death, they were trying to crush everything inside my neck. His force was so overwhelming I felt myself trying to slip to the floor just to make it more difficult for him to hold me up by gripping my neck with such power.

Teddy Byrnes was screaming the way the old Celtic warriors supposedly had. It was said they could half-paralyze their victims with their voices alone. There was great abiding mad pleasure in the sounds.

I was losing consciousness so quickly I operated on instinct. Somehow my knee came straight up. Somehow it reached its target. Somehow my power was enough to temporarily mitigate his power.

Dizzy, gagging, stumbling I searched the dark floor for my forty-five. He was behind me — I chanced looking back — bent over and clutching himself.

I knew it would be only seconds before he charged me again. I wouldn't have time to find my gun unless I literally stumbled over it.

A small metal statue of some presumably prominent figure stood on an end table. The head was so narrow it was almost pointed. I grabbed it just as the screaming started again.

The charge was pretty much the same kind of tackle-line maneuver he'd tried before. A mistake on his part. I knew when to step out of range. I also knew enough when to sink the statue in his forehead.

Between his rage and his shock and his pain he was temporarily disoriented. He staggered around, arms flailing for balance. The white T-shirt he wore was bloody from his hands swiping it.

I used the time to find my gun.

When I saw it I moved as fast as I could. It was under the coffee table.

And it was then that Byrnes decided to remind me of who and what he was. While I was grasping for the forty-five he got me around the hips, threw me over his shoulder and then heaved me into the fireplace. Bone and stone do not mix, not when bone is hurled against it at a great rate of speed.

Then he was pounding on me.

I hadn't had time to climb to my feet so he stood over me punching at will. Stomach, sternum, face, skull. This was the pattern he'd no doubt found most successful and most efficient. He was not a dumb man. Stomach, sternum, face, skull.

I kept rolling left and right, deflecting as many punches as I could.

The formula he'd been using must have gotten boring for him because he suddenly felt the need to pick me up and hurl me again, this time halfway across the width of the fireplace and into the stand of tools including the hand-tooled poker.

He looked as surprised as I felt when I was able to creak to my feet and grab the poker.

He'd been ready for another round of stomach-sternum-face-skull or some variation thereof when I waved the sharp-edged poker in front of me. He didn't move, just watched.

I moved several feet away from the fireplace. He stood where I'd just been.

"You're doing a lot better than I thought you would, Counselor."

"Thanks for the compliment. You're not doing quite as well as I thought you would."

"C'mon, now, Counselor, you're not dumb enough to think this is really over yet. Are you?"

"No, I guess it probably isn't."

And once again he showed me why he was Byrnes and I was McCain.

He bent down and snatched up the fireplace shovel from among the other scattered iron instruments. Now it was his turn to cut through the air with it. He used both hands the way he'd swing a baseball bat. None of this candy-ass McCain nonsense of just waving it through the air to keep him away.

I'd been playing defense. Byrnes, of course, was playing offense.

In this brief respite I had time to realize that I was in some real pain and that my nose was streaking blood into my mouth. The surprise was that I did not have a headache.

I kept thinking of the gun. The gun could save me. I couldn't think of anything else that could.

He lunged. I backed up three steps into a grandfather clock in a corner. The chimes went wild for a minute or so.

He smiled. He was probably playing a movie in his head. The best scenes would be me on the floor and him savaging my head with his iron shovel. Maybe when I was at least half gone he'd take my poker from me and bash what little remained of my life with my own weapon.

Oh, yeah. He'd been rejuvenated. The baseball bat swing came closer and closer. Backing me up. Making me stumble not once but twice. Enjoying himself because he got to see that he was in control again.

I was now on a path to reach the couch. He was pushing me to reach it, slashing the air when I tried to move in a different direction, leaving me no room to maneuver. I needed to get the gun under the coffee table.

Then it was my turn. Or I hoped it was. I attacked him. My turn to carve my own direction. Fuck him.

And it worked.

His response to my sudden strike was to swing in an ever wider arc and that left him off balance. And that was when the hook of my poker caught him on the right cheek. It wasn't a particularly sharp edge but I had the opportunity to hit him three quick times along the eye as well.

Blood poured from the massive cut I'd inflicted. His eyes lost focus for a few seconds.

I risked one more slash. It didn't cut but it disoriented him enough to lose his grip on his shovel.

He came at me but I'd been able to run around to the front of the couch.

I had half-ass good luck.

I wasn't quick enough to avoid the kicks he leveled at me as my hand scrabbled under the coffee table. He had to be wearing steel-toed boots. But I was quick enough to fill my hand with the gun so that when he grabbed me again — to hurl me across the room again? — I turned and shot him in the right shoulder. His hand shot out for the gun. He had the strength to wrench it out of my hand and it went off again. This time a bullet blasted his right thigh.

His first response was disorientation. He didn't cry out at the pain. He didn't try to shield himself from another shot. He just stood there staring at me in disbelief.

This wasn't the way his world was supposed to run. He was attacker, not victim. The other guy was supposed to be in pain.

Then he tried to reach me with his other arm.

I walked over to a brown leather armchair and sat down.

"Where's the heroin?" The trips to Mexico, packing the shipments privately. And heroin being the most profitable. I just took a guess.

He was starting to cry now. But as I soon found out, it wasn't because of pain. Not physical pain anyway. He careened around to the front of the couch and just let himself fall down on it. His eyes were closed for a second. No tears though. The crying I'd heard was in his throat.

"I go up again I won't be with my mom when she dies."

So easy to mock him. But I didn't. He was fading fast. His head wobbled and his breath came in gasps. He tried to reach up with the hand of the wounded shoulder and he sobbed.

"I always promised her." But that was all he muttered.

"Where's the heroin you and Anders ship?"

Drifting off: "Shoulda killed you."

Then: Sirens. Nearby. On the wooded trail.

A single siren now, coming this way.

It was enough to rouse Byrnes, but not for long. He was bleeding badly from both wounds. He mumbled something angry that I didn't understand.

I ran to the door and threw it open.

Chief Foster's car slid across the grass, stopping about ten feet from the house.

Then he was running with his own gun ready.

Then somebody else was exiting the car.

Mary; Mary Lindstrom; my Mary.

22

More sirens, this time including an ambulance. But also three more cars from the police station, including Sheila Kelly, the forensic expert Foster had brought with him from his last job. Within five minutes of striding through the door with a large black bag, she had found the subbasement where all the shipping equipment was placed on a Formica work table along with two sizable bags of heroin to be shipped to Anders's buyers.

Mary had called Foster and explained where I'd gone and why. He had picked her up immediately and brought her here.

Now Mary, Foster, and I talked on the front porch.

Foster wore a short-sleeved yellow shirt and brown trousers. "The drugs explains how Anders could live so well."

"And why he had to force Al Carmichael out. Carmichael would never have put up with using the company as a ruse for shipping drugs."

"I don't understand why a man like Steve Donovan would have, either."

"I don't think he did. Not at first. I think he probably found it out after Anders had been at it for some time. Donovan had political aspirations for one thing. And for another he loved that company. He and Carmichael had turned it into a going operation. I'm pretty sure he confronted Anders and Anders made a promise to stop but then never did. And that's why the two were always arguing all the time. And that's why Anders killed Donovan."

He smiled at Mary. "Mary and I had a little talk while we were racing out here."

"All I told him, Sam, was that I was at least *willing* to consider the possibility that Will was guilty."

The night went on. Bird racket in the trees; rain wind slamming against the windows and chilling us on the porch; animals scurrying for shelter before the rain itself began.

I sat there briefly comforted by nature because there would be no comfort coming from Foster.

"So even after all this you still don't think Anders killed him?"

"As I said to Mary, Sam, why would he? He didn't know how to run the company. With Donovan gone it would become obvious that the whole operation was getting a fair share of its profits from an unknown source. The IRS would have a lot of questions and pretty soon after that they'd get real suspicious and kick it over to the FBI. And then Anders would be all over."

"Maybe Anders didn't have any choice except to kill him."

Mary looked pained that I'd rushed past Foster's take on Anders to go right back into mine.

I said, "Maybe Anders was afraid that Donovan had finally had enough. That he was going to go to the authorities and tell them everything."

"He'd be willing to sacrifice his political career?"

"Donovan had a terrible temper and he could be a bully when he got sanctimonious but generally he was an honorable man. He had to be miserable every day of his life knowing what Anders was up to. So I could see him snapping, saying that he'd had enough. Figuring out the best case he could for himself so maybe — just possibly — he could tell the law everything and avoid prison. Put everything on Anders, where it belonged anyway."

"It seemed to me that Senator O'Shay had gotten Donovan pretty fired up about becoming a congressman."

From the front doorway, Sheila Kelly said, "Think I could borrow you for a little while, Chief?"

"Be right with you," Foster said, standing up. "We're pretty much done here with you folks, Sam, if you'd like to go home."

"I asked Mrs. Nelson to watch the girls. She's usually in bed by nine thirty and it's almost that time."

"You know where to reach us, Chief."

After a clumsy handshake, I said, "I'm still going to prove that Anders killed Donovan."

His smile went to Mary, not me. "And I'm still going to prove he didn't kill Donovan."

The rain came as soon as we reached the highway. I kept the radio off so we could hear it play on the roof. Mary had her head back, eyes closed. Headlights were all we could see of the oncoming cars till they passed us.

"I was afraid you'd be mad at me, Sam."

"You love me. You were afraid for me. You wanted to protect me."

"If I ever need a lawyer I'll hire you. You made a very nice defense of me." Then, "So now will you tell me what happened with

Byrnes back there?"

Foster had apologized to Mary but said he wanted to question me alone. He started by saying that even though I'd technically broken the law by entering the cabin without any kind of permission or warrant, he was grateful for what I'd done and no charges would be filed against me. I thanked him.

I hadn't had time to tell Mary about the confrontation with Teddy Byrnes. But now that I repeated what I'd told Foster I realized how easily the situation could have turned out the other way around. Byrnes was not only a psychopath but also a skilled thug. The two things that saved me were his blind hatred of me, which had led him to make bad decisions in his attempt to kill me, and my ability to stay cool enough to think through how to outplay him.

"I can't believe you're still alive. Aren't you in pain?"

"Yeah. My right side hurts quite a bit."

"And you don't have a headache?"

"Just now starting to. But it's not bad."

"A big drink and right to bed for you."

"I need to unwind."

"All right. A big drink and then you unwind."

"This'll all be on the news. I wonder what

the girls'll make of it."

"They'll be proud. They'll make you tell them all about tonight. The cleaned-up version, of course."

"That should be an interesting version. I don't even get to mention the hookers?"

"What hookers?"

"See how fast that got your attention? Any kind of story you're telling, you can never go wrong with hookers."

"Didn't we learn that in seventh grade?"

"No," I said, "I think it was eighth."

Since it was a workday I went to the office.

I did not stop anywhere along the way. Half of the front page of the morning paper dealt with the arrest of Lon Anders and the hospitalization of Teddy Byrnes. Valerie Donovan said that she would have no comment on the relationship between her husband and Anders. Chief Foster thanked me for my help with the case and called me "courageous." There was a photo of me looking like a sixteen-year-old. I'd never seen it before.

TV and radio people had shown up at the house around eight o'clock. The girls watched them from the front window. Kate kept asking me if she would get to be on TV.

Mary did a fine job as my public-relations representative. In her blue skirt with the blue buttons running down the right side and her smart white collarless blouse, her makeup modest and perfect, she cordially explained that I would be making a statement very soon but that I had other matters to deal with and right now just couldn't afford the distraction.

The word "hero" must have been used twenty times in the eight or nine minutes Mary was on the front porch. I was obviously no hero.

I hadn't expected to find Teddy Byrnes at Anders's house so you couldn't say I'd sought him out. And as much as I hated him, I hadn't been fighting him to rid humanity of a scourge; I'd just been trying to save my own sorry ass. But you couldn't say that to the press. To them you were a good guy or a bad guy, and if you were a good guy you just had to be heroic in some way.

When Mary came back inside, she said, "You now have a fan club."

"I don't want a fan club."

Kate said, "What's a fan club?"

Nicole said, "That's when people have posters of famous people on their walls and buy their records and stuff."

Kate said, "Have you made a record, Sam?"

So now I sat at my desk smoking more Luckies than I should have and popping aspirins every hour on the hour. My left arm hurt when I extended it and my right side ribs hurt when I so much as took a deep breath.

Jamie said, "Everybody's talking about you, Sam. I'm really proud."

"This'll last about two days and then my fifteen minutes'll be up."

"Look at that stack of phone messages and it's not even ten thirty."

"I looked at them. And they make me mad."

"Why would they make you mad?" Today Jamie wore a blue-and-white polkadot dress and a blue barrette that accented the appeal of her fetching Midwestern face and body.

"Because half these people wouldn't ever have returned my calls if last night hadn't happened."

"They just want to congratulate you."

"The only ones I'm returning are the ones that might mean a little business for us. I've been thinking of adding a security service for businesses. We don't have a local one. Some of the people who called probably need help that way."

"Boy, you never mentioned that before."

"I need to make more money. I . . ." I hesitated. I wanted to hear myself say it. "I hope I'm getting married."

She had a great kid-sister grin. "That is so cool. Mary is the best woman you've ever been with."

"It took me a long time to realize that."

"I love her girls, too. I see them whenever I take my daughter to things for kids. Kate is hilarious."

I'd missed one of the phone slips. Now I sat staring at it. "This one I just saw."

"Whose is it?"

"Senator O'Shay."

"I didn't like him at all. He made me repeat his name and number three times and then he said, 'This is urgent government business, young woman.' "

"The hell it is. He heard my name on the radio and now he wants me to travel around with him while he's campaigning."

"I didn't like him before anyway. It really burns me up that his two sons don't have to serve when he's so big on the war."

"He's not going to win."

"You really think so?"

Her phone rang and by the face she made it had to be O'Shay. I shook my head.

"I'm sorry, Senator, he hasn't come in yet."

She held the receiver out while he ranted. He went through his "official government business" and then he wanted to know where he could find me and then he said, "A secretary in Washington would have done everything she could to find him. She'd have him on the phone by now. But that's a level of competence you're clearly not capable of."

I grabbed my receiver and said, "Look, you clown. You have no right to talk to her that way and I want you to apologize to her right now."

"Just who the hell are you to call me a clown?"

"I'm nobody, but I'm calling you a clown anyway."

"I'll be damned if I apologize to some stupid little —"

"You're going to lose, Senator. Big time. And Jamie and I are going to celebrate your defeat."

I slammed the phone down.

Jamie gave me a round of applause.

"You defended my honor, Sam. That was very sweet. Thank you."

"Just call me Sir Galahad."

"See — you *can't* take a compliment."

One of our five or six friendly running arguments.

I spent the next thirty-five minutes on the phone. The last call I made was to the hospital psych ward. The extremely friendly nurse I talked to — I'd said my name right at the top and she responded the way most people do to real live heroes — said that she'd talk with Dr. Rattigan about me visiting Will. And that, by the way, Will was now speaking haltingly but rationally and that Dr. Rattigan was very happy about this. She would call me back as soon as she could reach him. I used my best heroic voice to thank her. This hero stuff came in handy.

Karen called just before noon. "I spent an hour with Will this morning. He's almost Will again. I'll let him tell you what happened the other night. He absolutely didn't kill Donovan. He's worried now that he might have given Foster the idea that he was confessing or something. He'll want to talk to you about that."

"I hope to be up there this afternoon. The nurse I spoke with said she'd check with Rattigan. If Rattigan says no, I'll call Lindsey Shepard."

After a pause she said, "I'm going to forgive him, Sam. I love him. I'd planned on forgiving him but last night I got bitter all over again. I want to make our marriage work." And then she started talking about where I'd been last night. And what I'd done. And how she was so proud of me.

The nurse called me twenty minutes later. I was slotted in at four o'clock to see Will.

Greg Egan was waiting for me, his wheelchair pulled up to the table he favored in "Mike's," a sandwich shop three blocks from my office. Waiting with him was Ted Franks. Their bitter joke was that if they put together the legs Greg had lost in Nam and the right arm Ted had lost there, they'd have a pretty tough guy.

Greg had contacted me about a call he'd gotten from Senator O'Shay. He wanted to know if he should go to the press about it. He'd also talked to Will on the phone this morning. That made two reasons I'd been eager for this lunch.

"Hell," Ted said, "expose the bastard. You'd be doing all of us a favor."

Ted had a long, intense face sitting atop a lanky body. These days his empty right sleeve — he always wore long sleeves — was pinned to his shirt. As a Jew he'd always felt like an outsider in Black River Falls, he'd confessed over too many bottles of Bud one night, but oddly enough he felt that his

270

wound had given him the kind of friendship and acceptance he'd never had before.

Mike's was small, the air conditioning kept it at freezer level, and the clamorous crowd loved to shout appreciation to Mike Feldman for the quality of his numerous deli sandwiches. The shouts (and Mike's return shouts) were part of the ritual.

It got a lot worse if a Cubs game was on the radio. Mike Feldman was one of their messianic fans.

"So this asshole O'Shay calls me and says he'll be giving a speech at the steel plant in Cedar Rapids. He wants to have a vet on-stage with him. What he means is he needs a cripple. There're plenty of vets we know who like O'Shay and would be glad to do it for him. But they're not gimps."

Greg liked that word. The self-contempt seemed to give him pleasure. I'd given him one of my lectures one day but he'd told me to fuck off and I had.

"Think I should call the paper about it? Expose him?"

Ted said, "I think he should, but then I know how Denise feels about it so I should keep my big mouth to myself."

"Denise is against it?"

"You know her, Sam. She's had kind of a tough time with the way I am." In war times

271

vets' wives are always portrayed as the relentlessly optimistic vessels of support and good cheer for their husbands. But there are of course wives who have many of the same adjustment problems as their husbands. Denise Egan was one of them.

"I'm with Denise."

My words surprised him. "Really? I know how much you hate O'Shay. This could really make trouble for him."

"First of all, Greg, all he did was ask you if you'd appear with him. The thing about 'gimps,' as you like to call yourself, is in your mind as far as proving anything. He didn't even hint at it. I doubt anybody in the press would even be interested in it. And second of all, think about Denise. Like Ted said, it's easy for us to tell you what to do. And it'd be great if you could do some damage to O'Shay, but it wouldn't be great for Denise. You know how much she hates talking to reporters. Now let's talk about Will. How did he sound when you talked to him?"

"Believe it or not, he sounded like Will. He's a little slower than usual — you know how he likes jokes — but he's definitely Will again." Then, "But he's a little weird about Karen." He glanced at Ted as he said this.

Ted said, "We started telling him how lucky he was to have Karen and all he said was that he hoped she'd understand some-day. Then he changed the subject right away."

"It kind of sounded like he'd said good-bye or something," Ted said.

"Yeah, like he was moving on."

"Maybe he's not as back together as we think he is. Maybe he was just saying that he hopes that Karen understands all he's put her through. He has to be feeling at least a little guilty about things."

"That's for sure," Ted said. "All the shit my wife and kids've had to put up with while I adjusted to not having a right arm."

"I'm the same with Denise and my kids. I feel guilty for not being able to walk. It's ir-rational but I can't help it. I see other dads playing ball with their kids —"

He started to choke up but stopped him-self.

There was just no doubt about it.

War was fucking wonderful. Just think of all the parades. Just think of all the medals.

Just think of all the O'Shays.

23

He smiled as soon as he saw me.

He sat in the same chair he'd been in when I visited him before but now he was dressed in the kind of shirt and trousers he'd wear under his white medical jacket at the veterinary clinic. No Sears for him.

The room was filled with late afternoon sunshine and the heavy blue smoke of his cigarettes. "Well, look at you, Sam. If you were just a couple feet taller you'd look like an adult."

Strained, but better than the eerie state of withdrawal he'd been in since the murder.

I sat on the edge of the bed. "Had lunch with Greg and Ted. Greg said you sounded a whole lot better."

"Yeah, I do."

The first minutes of conversation had come easily for him. But now the mouth pinched and the eyes narrowed and he sighed shakily. When he started to speak it was in the slow, precise way that Greg had described.

"I was sitting at home after the ER and I just kept thinking of how much I wanted to be part of the group again. I didn't really get a chance to express myself at the party — at least as I remember it; I was sort of hammered — so I guess I got it in my head that if I could talk to Steve — just the two of us — he'd see why I'd joined that anti-war group. And then I'd tell him that I was dropping it. And then we'd be friends again. Not just Steve but everybody. Buddies. That's all I could think of.

"So I called Cherie's where Steve hangs out a lot to see if he was there. He was, so I drove out there. He didn't want to have anything to do with me so I kept on knocking them down and finally I made it to my car somehow — it was practically parked in the woods — and I passed out. And when I woke up the parking lot was almost empty. I got out to take a leak — I was still pretty drunk — and that was when I saw Donovan on the ground. I was so wobbly I remember almost falling over him. Then somebody hit me from behind across the back of my head and it was maybe half an hour later before I came to."

"Do you remember calling me from home

earlier?"

"Yeah. I was having a really bad panic attack and I didn't know what to do. I thought maybe you could help me. But as soon as I hung up I thought maybe the best thing to do would be to go out to Cherie's and talk to Donovan. What a stupid idea that turned out to be. Man, I remember trying to drive home after I found the body. I was so terrified I couldn't keep the car on the road. I even got so confused at one point I wondered if I really had killed him but couldn't remember. It was like being in the psych hospital again. Days when I couldn't think clearly. I pulled off the road to the place where the police found me. I know Foster still thinks I killed Donovan but I didn't."

"I know that, Will. And so does Karen."

His cheeks tinged red suddenly. His eyes closed and he swayed forward, then checked himself. He had to clear his throat to speak. "I'm going to say something you won't want to hear, Sam."

I waited him out.

"I've given this a lot of thought. I know how much I owe Karen. And I don't have to tell you how much I love our daughter. But the thing is —" He wrung his hands. His gaze fled to the window. "The thing is that I think I've had such a hard time adjusting after coming back home because the marriage isn't right, Sam. And that's not Karen's fault and it's not mine."

I still said nothing.

A big dopey grin. "There's this young woman I hired, Sam. And she's been with me now for —"

Oh God. At least four married friends of mine had laid The List on me over the years. They wanted my approval, even permission in a strange way. I barely listened to Will's List. I knew it by heart.

She's just so much fun. My marriage hasn't been fun like this in a long time.

She makes me feel younger. I even look younger when I'm shaving in the morning.

She has these ideas for my business. She's my lover but she's also like this brilliant thinker.

I know what it'll be like for my little daughter — I know how selfish I'm being — but kids get over it eventually.

It'll be tight for a while money-wise with the settlement and all — her fucking lawyer is an assassin — but I can ride that out, too.

And did I mention the sex? I swear to God I got it up three times the other night. I haven't done that for years.

"I didn't want it to happen. It's just that April —"

"Her name is April?"

277

"What the hell, Sam. Is there something wrong with being called April? It's a pretty name."

"I was just surprised is all. April, I mean."

"I know what you're doing here."

"Doing? What're you talking about?"

"You're taking Karen's side. You're making me the bad guy."

"No, I'm not." But I was. All Karen had done for him.

April.

"If you sat down and talked to her for a few minutes you'd see what a sharp girl she is. And you'd like her. And not just because she's so pretty. She came up and saw me yesterday and I have this whole different mindset. Don't I sound happy?"

He did. Given the fact that he was still the number one suspect in a homicide, he sounded ridiculously happy.

"Karen knows you had an affair with Cathy Vance. She found those letters you wrote her."

"Yeah, I know. And I don't blame her for being hurt."

"That's big of you."

"Cut me some slack here, man. Look at all I've been through."

He was feeling sorry for himself but he deserved to, the poor, suffering, aggravating bastard.

"What's the point of writing all these letters and then not mailing them?"

A shrug. "Oh, you know, most of them are so sentimental they're sort of embarrassing. But they made me feel better just writing them. I probably should've thrown them away."

"So when does Karen get the news?"

"I'm not ready to tell her yet. This whole thing with Foster has to be cleared up. And then we have to wait a while because April has to tell her husband and she's a little bit afraid."

"You didn't mention she was married."

"This is pretty complicated. She's not telling anybody about it and neither am I. Karen's coming up in an hour and bringing a sandwich from Mike's deli. It's tempting to tell her but I won't. I'm just so damned happy, Sam, I had to tell somebody. I got so caught up in the anti-war thing I just stayed drunk and fucked up my life totally. Now I have a special reason to get this Donovan thing over with."

This Donovan thing. A small but annoying problem. Who hasn't been accused of murder?

"I was thinking maybe you'd forgotten about that. What with April and all."

"God, Sam, are you mocking me?"

"A little."

We were silent for a time.

"We still friends, Sam?"

"Yeah, but you piss me off for Karen's sake."

"And you of all people don't have any right to judge me. All the affairs you've been in and out of."

"But I wasn't married."

He was quick.

"Sounds like that's about to change."

"Yeah, it is."

"Great. You should've married Mary a long time ago. How about we both be happy for each other?"

Damn him. I cared about him and I'd stand by him no matter what. I hadn't heard him this happy since he'd come back from Nam.

"Are you still sure Anders killed Donovan?" he asked.

"Yeah. But even after last night with the heroin, Foster still doesn't think he had a motive to kill him."

"Maybe he was afraid that Donovan was going to the feds."

"That's what I told him. But no sale."

"We just need to figure this damned thing out."

"Yeah, I guess 'we' do."

"You're mocking me again."

I was. What he was about to do to Karen and Peggy Ann still pissed me off.

"Not really. I'm irritated with you and I'm irritated with me. I'm being a judgmental asshole and you're not concerned enough with Foster. He still wants to put you in prison for life."

From the door I said, "Will, you need to think back through the whole night. Concentrate on every single thing you can remember from the time you left your house to the time the police found you in your car. You said somebody knocked you out. Really focus on that. There may have been some little thing you've overlooked. You can be a big help to me."

"I'm sorry, Sam. You've been working so hard for me. I really appreciate it. You know I do."

I nodded. "Yeah; yeah, I do."

O'Shay got his gimp.

I felt sorry for the kid, obviously. He appeared to be about fourteen years old, the Irish altar-boy type right down to his freckles and brief nose. They were on a platform so heavy with American flags I was surprised it didn't crash to the ground. This was a nooner; employees at a steel plant in Cedar Rapids had been treated to free hot dogs and burgers and soft drinks over their lunch hour in exchange for putting up with twenty minutes of lies and patriotic treacle. Pure TV.

"I swear to you, this young man's fate will be avenged. We will never allow barbarians like the Vietcong to slaughter and wound our troops. The anti-American crowd says that we should stop 'carpet-bombing,' that we're killing too many *innocent* Vietnamese. What they're too stupid to realize is that there is no such thing as an innocent Vietnamese. Young or old, they all have one thing in common: they hate Americans — we went there to help them, after all — and won't be happy until we're all dead."

A funny thing happened to the ear-shattering applause that should've followed such a red meat line. Maybe it was because the workers were holding hot dogs or burgers or soft drinks and couldn't manipulate their hands to make the resounding noise O'Shay was used to. But even the poor kid in the wheelchair didn't show much outward enthusiasm for O'Shay's psycho remarks. Even if the kid was pro-war, he'd been there and seen a good number of innocent Vietnamese.

I got up and walked over to the TV and clipped it off.

Mary came back with an ice-cold bottle of Hamm's for me. She'd been upstairs with the kids. I'd tried it, but given my mood I wasn't much company. I did get an especially wet kiss from Kate which I hadn't earned and a compliment on my two-day-old haircut from sweet, sensible Nicole.

"Feeling any better?"

"Afraid not. Thanks for putting up with me." She had brought a can of 7UP along for herself. She curled up beside me on the couch. "Is it Karen you're feeling bad for?"

"It's everything. Foster's obsession with Will and Anders getting off on a murder charge and Karen, sure, of course. I don't know how she'll handle it."

Mary kissed me on the cheek and took my hand. "How about we just sit here and try to relax?"

For the next hour we watched a rerun of *The Untouchables.* As much as I liked the show occasionally, I never understood the American public's fondness for gangster lore. Predators who prey on weak and defenseless people didn't exactly make me want to spend much time with them, especially when they were as stupid as most gangsters are. Cunning, yes, but most of them — with the exception of the grand eccentric Bugsy Siegel — don't make for riveting drama. Unless you're into bloodbaths. I'd graced Mary with this sour speech a few times before. She deserved to be spared tonight.

When the call came, I was just about to head for home.

"It's Karen, Sam. Will must have decided to tell her about this April tonight. She just keeps sobbing and sobbing. You really need to go over there."

I went.

24

Karen greeted me in a wrinkled — Karen in something wrinkled! — white blouse and red walking shorts. In her left hand was a Chesterfield and in her right a very dark drink. It was now ten minutes after nine.

"I didn't expect you to come over."

"Mary's worried about you and so am I."

Her eyes were reddened from crying but she was apparently more in control of herself than she'd been on the phone with Mary. "I haven't seen Peggy Ann in two days. I just don't want her to see me this way. Thank God for my sister. I'm so damned selfish."

"Yeah, that's you. Selfish."

"Let me get you a beer."

There were at least two ashtrays overflowing. There was a water ring from a glass on the mahogany coffee table. A blue-covered throw pillow had fallen on the floor. A section of the newspaper hung from the phone stand. In a fair number of homes this would be normal everyday life. But in Karen's case this signaled breakdown.

After handing me my bottle of Hamm's, she walked over to the couch and sat down. I admired her most excellent legs and waited for her to talk.

She began by patting a small stack of papers next to her. "I'm going to try very hard not to cry."

"Cry all you want, Karen. Seriously. You've helped me through some real bad nights of my own."

"I'm sick of crying, Sam. And now I'm sick of trying to save this marriage."

So he had told her.

"I went to see him tonight and he acted like everything was fine. I know you were there earlier. Anyway, by the time I left there he was almost like his old self."

So he hadn't told her.

"Then I got home and I made the mistake of going in his den again. Since I found those letters I've become compulsive about it. It's as if I've conditioned myself to distrust him. As far as I know, he was faithful to me all the time we were married up until he got back from Vietnam. Maybe he's 'acting out,' as the man at the VA told us. I didn't find anything in his den tonight but when I looked in the front closet I saw this valise I bought him for his birthday a few years ago. It was leaning against the wall so I picked it up."

She paused to sit up very straight and to take a deep, deep breath. Then she picked up the sheaf of papers. "He has a new girlfriend. I shouldn't say girlfriend — he tells her he wants to marry her."

I wanted to hate him but I couldn't. The war had destroyed him. The old Will, the good, compassionate, clear-thinking Will had been killed along with the little girl his bullets had ripped apart.

She held them out to me. "Please take these, will you, Sam? Read them. See how far gone he is."

I knew what I'd find in the papers. April. But I had no idea how I'd respond.

I got them all right and I came back and sat down and put them in my lap all right but I didn't read them. Not right away. Because when I *did* read them she was going to ask me if he'd said anything about the woman he was writing to. And if I lied to her and she later found out that I'd lied to her she would never trust me again.

She lighted anther cigarette but it took three angry little attempts to make her silver lighter light. But it wasn't the lighter that wasn't doing well, it was her.

"Read the one on top, Sam. Even when we were first going out he didn't say things like that to me."

Now I lighted a cigarette. It took me two matches.

I lifted the top white sheet of typing paper and read the first paragraph.

You're my first thought in the morning and my last at night. At first you were only my heart, but now you are my soul as well.

I had the semi-serious idea that he'd found an article or even a little paperback that listed all the things a love song should contain.

And it went on that way for the entire page. If there was a romantic cliché he missed, I couldn't find it. I tried not to think, cliché or no cliché, of the effect all the cornball language would have on poor Karen.

I raised my head and when our eyes met, I shook my head. She started crying then.

"Read a few more. See what I'm up against."

"Oh, I think I've got the idea here good enough, Karen."

Crying more now. "Please just read a few more. Look how much he loves her."

"You're punishing yourself, Karen. I don't

want to help you."

"Just get to the one where he says he wants to have children. Children — I don't know how he could even think of such a thing. Isn't Peggy Ann enough for him?"

The children reference was not in the next letter nor the next one nor the next one. But there in the middle of the following one was that word — "children" — and it might as well have been in neon. Yup, he and April would have a whole passel of wee ones and they would live somewhere over the rainbow and speak only in the language of the worst romance novels. And their wee ones would speak the same language, too, and in time have their own passel of treacle-speaking wee ones. What he was outlining was the hammiest Broadway musical ever created.

But then I glanced down a few lines and when I saw that partial sentence I realized that Will had lied to me.

"I'm so sorry, Karen."

I had a difficult time not bursting out the door. I really needed to get going.

I put the papers down. "I want to call Mary. All right if I use the phone in the kitchen?"

"Of course."

She didn't seem curious about why I didn't use the phone in the living room.

I kept my voice low.

"She's in terrible shape, Mary. I don't think she should be alone. Would it be all right for her to stay with you tonight?"

"Of course. God, I can't imagine what she's going through."

It took a full fifteen minutes to persuade Karen to spend the night at Mary's but finally she agreed. And finally, still expressing second thoughts, she put some things in a small blue canvas bag and we went out to my car. Where she expressed third thoughts before actually getting inside.

On the way to Mary's she said she was acting like a child and that was undoubtedly why I was treating her like one. Then she kind of sank into herself and said she was so tired she could barely keep her eyes open.

I made sure that Karen was in the safe and comforting presence of Mary and then I was in my car and speeding away.

25

One light burned in the Victorian house that stood silhouetted in the moonlight, all turrets and gables and broken roof lines. The light was on the first floor front where the waiting area was.

I saw all this as I stood next to my car, which I'd parked half a block away in a residential neighborhood just now bedding down for the night. I didn't want to announce my visit.

I kept to the shadows cast by streetlights and heavily leafed trees. Now would be an inconvenient time for Foster — or any of his force, for that matter — to show up because I had my forty-five jammed down the beltline of my trousers.

I walked wide when I got to the cross street where the Victorian lay. There were no other houses or buildings on either side of it for half a block or so. I didn't want anybody to see me approaching, though with the upstairs apartment lights out I wasn't sure anybody was home. I went down half a block and then walked back using a long windbreak of pines as cover.

In back of the Victorian was an asphalt parking area for clients. On the far side of the lot was a two-story garage. Using a side window, I could see that two cars were there. This didn't necessarily mean they were home. They were social people. Friends might have picked them up for the evening.

Then, my eyes adjusting to the gloom of the garage interior, I saw the two outsize suitcases standing next to the trunk of the smart black Oldsmobile.

I looked up at the dark windows on the back of the house. I wanted to be sure no one was watching me.

I went in through the side door of the garage. Smells of car oil and the mown-lawn scent from a small riding mower. I walked over to the Oldsmobile. Two dark traveling bags were laid across the back seat. I walked around to the trunk. The lid was a quarter open. Another traveling bag. The suitcases on the floor would be set in there and the traveling bag spread across them.

I wasn't looking at a vacation; I was looking at an escape.

I walked to the front of the car, opened the hood and took care of something. Then I closed the hood and left the garage.

I stood in the shadows of the terra cotta walls. The Oldsmobile undoubtedly belonged to Randall. The other car was a sleek red Mustang and had to be Lindsey's.

I eased the forty-five from the top of my pants and proceeded to the back door. As I'd hoped, it was unlocked. There would be a few more things to pack and take along.

Four steep steps leading to the interior.

Six steps before I could see well enough to know that I was in a storage area of some kind.

Ten steps to a door that opened on the familiar layout of the Shepard psychology practice.

They had both worked several intense years to build this practice and win it an admirable reputation. Now all that was left was furtive flight.

I walked as quietly as I could down the corridor of offices, the only light coming from the street. I listened for any sound that might tell me where they were but there were only the weary griefs that old houses, no matter how well you refurbish them, make late at night.

When I reached the front I stood in the

light I'd seen when I'd been standing next to my car. I was so used to darkness by now the light had a garish, almost obscene cast to it. A coat tree and a rubber runner for when winter came and a large closet door. And then, just out of the light, the reception desk and the furnishings for the clients.

I turned around and started toward the staircase that led to their apartment upstairs and there she was waiting for me. I could have stepped on her hand but by sheer luck I didn't. It was flung away from her body like something discarded.

Once again my eyes needed time to pick out detail in darkness.

I got down on one knee to look at her more carefully, shoving the forty-five back into my beltline.

A relaxed evening at home. Jeans and a Joni Mitchell T-shirt. Tiny bare feet. This was "April," better known as Lindsey. He'd wanted to exult over her with me but he'd known how I would respond if he told me that he'd fallen in love with his shrink. In the last letter of his I'd read, he'd referred to her as "trapped in the Victorian age." He'd obviously meant the house she shared with her husband.

The good doctor had shot her in the forehead twice. He hadn't taken any chances. The eyes reflected the horror. The body had begun to foul itself.

"The first time I ever saw her, she was fourteen years old. And I've been obsessed with her ever since." Then, "I want you to stand up with your arms straight in the air. You're not a very good burglar, McCain. I watched you the whole time you were in the back yard. I know you're carrying a gun. So I want the arms straight up in the air. Do you understand?"

"Uh-huh."

And I did. Before I could get to my own gun he could blow the back of my head off.

I stood up the way he'd told me to.

"Now take your gun out slowly and put it between the spindles on the stairs. You're an intelligent man and I assume you want to live. So be very careful."

At most times I would have found his clothes amusing. The professorial air had evolved into Western clothes. A dark shirt with white piping, tight jeans, and what appeared to be real lizard cowboy boots.

"You're looking at my clothes. I don't like them, either. One of the ways I tried to keep her interested was by following trends. I'm a piss-poor cowboy, wouldn't you say?" Then, "Now the gun, McCain."

As I did what he said, his self-mocking

tone gave way to melancholy. "If you're curious, her mother brought her to me when she was fourteen. I fell in love with her that very first day. I didn't care about anything but her. I had to put her in institutions three times before she was sixteen. She had an older brother she'd slept with since she was eleven and she believed she was in love with him. Her parents hadn't done anything about it until they finally came to me. By the time she was fifteen she'd come to be in love with me. I protected her as she'd never been protected before."

"And you were sleeping with her of course?"

"You have a way of being very ugly, McCain. Lindsey said the same thing about you." Then, "My loving her saved her. I made sure she finished high school with good grades and I saw her through college. We lived together all that time. Her parents had divorced and she despised them. The only trouble we had was when her brother secretly contacted her and she sneaked off to spend a weekend with him. Then everything started all over again. Fortunately I have an inheritance to rely on. I paid her brother quite a lot of money to never contact her again. I told him that if he ever tried, I'd have him killed. He believed me."

My gun now residing on the staircase, I began to wonder if this was his confession before he decided to kill me.

"So she was never on her own; and when she fell in love with Will Cullen and promised to marry him, you realized that this time she'd be gone for good."

"Oh, you don't think this was the first time, do you? I made the mistake of putting her through college so she could be a psychologist like me. We'd have a husband-and-wife practice and everything would be fine. But three different times she started sleeping with clients. Two of them happened to be married, so when I confronted them they agreed not to say anything. They wanted to save their marriages. One was single and he blackmailed me. I had to dig into my inheritance again. He had nothing to lose and he could have destroyed us. They'd all had backgrounds like hers; they'd been seriously molested. She identified with them. I always kept a close eye on any male she dealt with who'd been molested.

"Cullen was a war victim. I didn't think he was a prospect for her but I was very wrong, wasn't I? After the last one she promised that she'd never do it again. But she not only did it again, she fell in love with him. When I found out I started wondering how I could get rid of him. When I heard about the argument he'd had with Steve Donovan I saw my opportunity. I started following him around and the rest was pretty easy.

"But just a few hours ago she said she was going to call you and tell you everything, including that she was sure I'd killed Donovan. Then she told me that she hated me and he was going to leave his wife and that they were going to move from Black River Falls and get married. The other ones she'd slept with, she never talked about being in love with them. I think she believed she was healing them in some way — and healing herself as well. But this —"

He stopped talking and then he shot me twice.

For a second there was no pain and then there seemed to be nothing but pain and the blindness of injury, confusion and rage. I'd been hit just below my left shoulder and my right ribs.

I fell to my knees and then I fell to the floor.

Running; he was running hard through the house. He obviously assumed I was dead or soon would be anyway. Running. The back door opening and slamming.

I knew I wouldn't be conscious much longer. I needed to grab on to the lowest of the staircase spindles and somehow pull myself up. To my feet. The idea burned in my brain with the fever of a brilliant immortal thought. Of course. Get up and somehow make my way to the closest office.

It took three tries to get on my feet and what seemed like two or three hours to make it to the receptionist's desk and the telephone and even then when I got to the desk the first thing I did was fall across it and bang my chin hard against its surface.

But somehow the phone got in my hand and somehow I told 911 what had happened.

And just before I passed out I had the pleasure of hearing Randall Shepard trying to start his car. Grinding and grinding and grinding.

But he wasn't going anywhere.

Not without a distributor cap he wasn't.

I wasn't able to attend Steve Donovan's funeral. I was in the hospital. The docs were optimistic about my full recovery. As bad as being shot had been, my military accident had been much worse. I was surprised that I didn't have the headaches that had followed the crash. It was a damned nice surprise.

Kenny showed up a few times, as did Foster. My mom and sister called frequently. Two days into my stay I saw on the TV that Niven had passed. I wished I'd known him in his younger days. If even half the stories were true he would have been a hoot to have hung out with. And learned from.

I thought about Donovan some. He was the good-bad person most of us are but he'd taken his good-bad to epic size. He'd been a brave soldier and sometimes a generous man but I would never understand why he forsook Al Carmichael for a psychotic Anders.

As for Will and Karen, who knew? The only certain thing was that he'd need to find another psychologist.

I drifted in and out of sleep. Half the time I woke up I saw Mary sitting in a chair next to my bed smiling at me.

I remember one time she said, "You're a hero all over again. You're all over the news."

That wasn't what I wanted to hear so I didn't fight sleep this time. I dove deep into it.

The time I woke up just as they were bringing me my tiny, tiny dinner I got the best news of all, except the news that I was going to live, of course.

Mary said, "I just heard the news on the radio. There's a new poll. Senator O'Shay is eighteen points behind."

I laughed with the same boisterous pleasure I'd once reserved for Bugs Bunny cartoons. Eighteen points behind. There was, after all, a God.

ABOUT THE AUTHOR

Ed Gorman is the beloved author of dozens of mystery novels, including the *New York Times* bestseller *Frankenstein,* which he co-wrote with Dean Koonz. He has received the Shamus Award, the Spur Award, and the International Fiction Writers Award. Ed lives in Cedar Rapids, Iowa.

The employees of Thorndike Press hope you have enjoyed this Large Print book. All our Thorndike, Wheeler, and Kennebec Large Print titles are designed for easy reading, and all our books are made to last. Other Thorndike Press Large Print books are available at your library, through selected bookstores, or directly from us.

For information about titles, please call:
(800) 223-1244

or visit our Web site at:
http://gale.cengage.com/thorndike

To share your comments, please write:
Publisher
Thorndike Press
10 Water St., Suite 310
Waterville, ME 04901